THERE'S GUNPOWDER IN THE AIR

MANORANJAN BYAPARI

Translated from the Bengali by
ARUNAVA SINHA

eka

eka

Published in Bengali as *Batashe Baruder Gandha* in 2019 by Eka, an imprint of Westland Publications Private Limited

First published in English as *There's Gunpowder in the Air* in 2018 by Eka, an imprint of Westland Publications Private Limited

Published in English as *There's Gunpowder in the Air* in 2022 by Eka, an imprint of Westland Books, a division of Nasadiya Technologies Private Limited

No. 269/2B, First Floor, 'Irai Arul', Vimalraj Street, Nethaji Nagar, Allappakkam Main Road, Maduravoyal, Chennai 600095

Westland and the Westland logo are the trademarks of Nasadiya Technologies Private Limited, or its affiliates.

Copyright © Manoranjan Byapari, 2018
Translation Copyright © Arunava Sinha, 2018

Manoranjan Byapari asserts the moral right to be identified as the author of this work.

ISBN: 9789395073301

10 9 8 7 6 5 4 3 2 1

This is a work of fiction. Names, characters, organisations, places, events and incidents are either products of the author's imagination or used fictitiously.

All rights reserved

Typeset by Jojy Philip, New Delhi 110 015
Printed at Nutech Print Services, Faridabad

No part of this book may be reproduced, or stored in a retrieval system, or transmitted in any form or by any means, electronic, mechanical, photocopying, recording, or otherwise, without express written permission of the publisher.

Manoranjan Byapari was born in the mid-fifties in Barishal, former East Pakistan. His family migrated to West Bengal in India when he was three. They were resettled in Bankura at the Shiromanipur Refugee Camp. Later, they were forced to shift to the Gholadoltala Refugee Camp, 24-Parganas, and lived there till 1969. However, Byapari had to leave home at the age of fourteen to do odd jobs. In his early twenties, he came into contact with the Naxals and with the famous labour activist Shankar Guha Niyogi. Byapari was sent to jail during this time, where he taught himself to read and write. Later, while working as a rickshaw-puller in Kolkata, Byapari had a chance meeting with the renowned Bengali writer Mahasweta Devi, who urged him to write for her journal *Bartika*. He has written twenty-seven books since. Some of his important works include *Chhera Chhera Jibon*, *Ittibrite Chandal Jibon* (memoir), the Chandal Jibon trilogy (novels) and *Motua Ek Mukti Senar Naam*. Until 2018, he was working as a cook at the Hellen Keller Institute for the Deaf and Blind in West Bengal.

In 2018, the English translation of Byapari's memoir, *Ittibrite Chandal Jibon* (*Interrogating My Chandal Life*), received the Hindu Prize for non-fiction. In 2019, he was awarded the Gateway Lit Fest Writer of the Year Prize. Also, this English translation of his novel *Batashe Baruder Gandha* (*There's Gunpowder in the Air*) was shortlisted for the JCB Prize for Literature 2019, the DSC Prize for South Asian Literature 2019, the Crossword Book Award for Best Translation 2019 and the Mathrubhumi Book of the Year Prize 2020. He was appointed chairman of the newly instituted Dalit Sahitya Akademi in Bengal in 2020.

In 2021, Byapari was elected a member to the Bengal Legislative Assembly as a Trinamool Congress candidate.

Arunava Sinha translates classic, modern and contemporary Bengali fiction and non-fiction into English. Seventy-one of his translations have been published so far. Twice the winner of the Crossword translation award, for Sankar's *Chowringhee* (2007) and Anita Agnihotri's *Seventeen* (2011), respectively, and the winner of the Muse India translation award (2013) for Buddhadeva Bose's *When the Time is Right*, he has also been shortlisted for the Independent Foreign Fiction prize (2009) for his translation of *Chowringhee* and for the Global Literature in Libraries Initiative Translated YA Book Prize for his translation of Md Zafar Iqbal's *Rasha*, and longlisted for the Best Translated Book award, USA, 2018 for his translation of Bhaskar Chakravarti's *Things That Happen and Other Poems*. In 2021, his translation of Taslima Nasrin's *Shameless* was shortlisted for the National Translation Award in the USA. Besides India, his translations have been published in the UK and the US in English, and in several European and Asian countries through further translation.

Currently, he is an associate professor of practice in the Creative Writing department at Ashoka University, and Co-Director, Ashoka Centre for Translation.

AUTHOR'S NOTE

I was arrested by the police in late 1974 or early 1975. The charges included use of guns, use of bombs, disturbing the peace, and so on. I did have some connection with Naxals at this time, though the police did not know of it. They arrested me as a miscreant. Even the political party with which I had links did not consider me a party worker. To the police I was an antisocial goon. I used to consider myself a Naxal, as did my companions. But Naxals did not consider us one of them. They called us the lumpen proletariat.

The police arrested me early one morning at the place where I was hiding. I was taken to the police headquarters at Lalbazar and given the third degree. At first the police had expected to discover a huge stockpile of arms with me, but the officers were extremely disappointed when their search of the house I was arrested from yielded nothing.

They filed a number of cases against me, along with the thirty or so people they had arrested that day. It was in the lock-up in Lalbazar that I met Debashish Bhattacharya and

Kallol Sengupta. We were presented in Bankshall Court and sent to Alipur Special Jail as under-trial prisoners.

I was there for nearly two years, undergoing trial the entire period. Then I was released on bail for Rs 1000, after furnishing a bond of Rs 100. The trial continued for two years more, during which time I had to appear in court for hearings. Eventually the case against me was dismissed.

I heard many stories from my fellow prisoners during those two years in jail. There were some people there who kept coming back. Prison was like a home to them. They told me stories too. That was when I heard the story of the jailbreak attempted by Paritosh Banerjee and his fellow Naxals from the Panchanantala area of Calcutta.

I had no thoughts of being a writer at that time. When I did begin to write later, it occurred to me to write the stories I had heard in prison. That is what I have done here, only changing the names of the characters.

Manoranjan Byapari
1 November 2018

THE WORLD I HAVE SEEN IS WHAT I WRITE ABOUT

He appears to be about fifty, but is in fact far older. His moustache and hair are more grey than black now, his bright eyes radiate immeasurable curiosity. Manoranjan Byapari is a son of the soil. A writer, a former rickshaw-driver, and, since then, an able cook. He has no hesitation in identifying himself as a member of the Namasudra caste.

He wiped out the stigma of his own illiteracy in jail, driven by lofty ambition to embark on the journey of learning the alphabet at the age of twenty-four. This led to the highly unusual path of self-education that culminated in Byapari's becoming a writer. Describing his long solo voyage in his characteristically animated manner, he says, 'I was in jail then, in despair and unable to hide my anguish. That was when a man of about sixty became my confidante and inspired me in different ways. He had been convicted for cheating, which meant that this was his profession. You cannot succeed in this line of work unless you're very clever. It was a sort of game for him. He was the one who motivated me to become literate, explaining that educated convicts were given different kinds of work in jail that involved writing. This allowed them to practise their skills as well. But illiterate people could only be assigned physical labour. It was essentially on his advice that I taught myself to read through a very unusual process. This gradually opened up an unending horizon of knowledge.'

It was after this that Byapari began to read literature. 'The first book I read was Manoj Basu's novel *Nishikutumbo* (*Relatives by Night*), followed by Jarasandha's *Louhokopat* (*The Iron Gate*).' Released from jail soon afterwards, he went back to his old profession of being a rickshaw-driver, in the course of which he happened to meet the renowned writer Mahasweta Devi. This acquaintance developed into a relationship which transported him to a world of unknown wonders. 'It was on Mahasweta Devi's inspiration that I began to write. My first piece was published in her magazine *Bartika*. I was an avid reader back then, always asking people around me the meanings of words I could not decipher for myself. This was how I went from literacy to reading and, eventually, to attempting to write. The journey took six years.'

However, when Byapari began writing, it was under pseudonyms such as Madan Dutta, Arun Mitra, and Jeejibisha (the Bengali word for 'lust for life'). The intention of this expedition behind a concealed identity was self-examination. Enriched by the experiences of his community and his society, Byapari evolved into a writer, another Advaita Mallabarman, as it were. But he never wanted to position himself as a Dalit writer or as a citizen of the fourth world.

'After the break-up of the Soviet Union, I was convinced there are only two classes of people,' he says. 'As the old saying goes, the oppressor and the oppressed. Everyone is as tyrannical as they can be, and those who have no power suffer this in silence. But when the same people acquire power in some manner, they too exploit those who are less powerful than them. These things lead to issues that people revolt over, which in turn gives birth to leaders. In other words, the objective of human beings is to be authoritarian in one form or another. And in the course of fulfilling this objective, even those who are referred to as dalits become leading figures of society. There are plenty of examples of this. All it needs to be such a leading figure is money. It is only in the case of the poor and the illiterate that the question of caste comes up. No one cares about the caste of the wealthy, whose only identity is that they are rich.

'What do I say about myself in this situation? To a high caste person I'm a dalit, untouchable. To other dalits I'm a rickshaw-driver. To other rickshaw-drivers I'm a writer, and therefore untouchable as far as they are concerned. Those who are at the forefront of dalit movements now are educated people, even if they are low-caste individuals. Many of them are senior government officers, occupying high positions in the social hierarchy, in other words. They're playing out their leadership ambitions at the expense of dalits, to whom it makes no difference, for the dalit remains nothing more than a dalit. These leaders do not even consider their domestic servants human, and yet they're leading dalit movements. Of course there are a few exceptions, as there always are. But my experience with the majority of dalit leaders has not been satisfying.'

In the course of conversation, Byapari brings up stories about Birbal. He points out how a line can be made to look short by drawing a longer line next to it. He advises free-thinkers from his own community to be more generous, more hard-working, more class-conscious. Drawing on a series of examples from his own world, he speaks passionately about his life. And to tell his stories better, he picks up his pen, which is how his novels and his short stories are born. He has received very little help in publishing these. 'The first person to publish my book was Manoj Bandyopadhyay,' he says, 'and the first person who gave me an opportunity to write was Mahasweta Devi. Pranab Chakraborty has published as many as seven of my novels. The person who gave me a job is a brahmin too.' And so his definition of caste is unorthodox. He considers poverty the more important factor, for the caste of the rich man is immaterial. 'People who work for Bata make shoes for a profession, yet no one asks them about their caste. But the man who sits on a pavement knocking nails into the soles of shoes takes on the caste of a muchi, a cobbler. Economic status is what matters the most.'

Byapari went to Dandakaranya in 1971 as a refugee all over again. He made a number of visits to the place subsequently, especially during the 1980s, which was when he met Shankar Guha Niyogi and became part of his movement for workers' rights. He acquired several skills during this period, and built considerable experience in battling for rights. But when the movement collapsed after Guha Niyogi was murdered in 1991, he returned to Bengal, after which his life as a writer began.

And yet, Byapari has not been, and still isn't, overcome by despair. However, he acknowledges the class struggle, and believes that all humans have the desire to be masters of other humans. But he trusts the better sense of people as well, and in the final analysis, all his faith is centred on other human beings. He is a believer in human progress, who puts truth on a higher pedestal than caste differences, economic disparity and, most of all, the conflict between the oppressor and the oppressed. He paints familiar worlds in imaginative ways using truth as his palette. As he overcomes obstacles, his eyes grow brighter still, eyes that do not rely on the illusion of dreams, but on the desire to build a new world. The harvest of his vision is his writing.

'The world I have seen is what I write about,' he says. 'I write about my environment, about the conflicts of dalit life, about my encounters with Marxism and its applications, about all the people I have met and the incidents I have witnessed. My philosophy of truth has emerged through all of these.'

– From the journal *Review/Preview*

THERE'S GUNPOWDER IN THE AIR

ONE

Long and slow, the jail siren wails. It's a quarter to six in the morning. The siren going off at this time means that the headcount has tallied. All the prisoners locked up last night have been located. None of them has succeeded in slipping past the alert eyes of the state-employed guards to escape. The message in the slow tone of the siren is just that. It signals relief.

It is the first phase of the volcanic seventies. No jail in the country is a secure fort now. One prison after another has been crumbling like worm-infested rotting wood. They have been broken by a group of arrogant and audacious fire-eaters, who are known politically as Naxals. Defying rigorous security, smashing all administrative resistance, they are escaping from their confinement with impunity.

True, not everyone is able to escape. The prisoners who fail have to atone for their transgressions with their lives. But no one is deterred. To them, killing and dying are like games children play. No law or regimentation or repression can obstruct those who are not afraid of death.

It is because of these intrepid prisoners that the situation in the jail is extremely volatile. The tension is palpable, for who knows what might happen next? There's no telling what these firebrand youngsters will do.

One more night has passed. No, there has been no mishap. The strains of the siren are carrying the message everywhere. For now, the jail authorities are freed of their anxiety.

The newly appointed jailer Bireshwar Mukherjee has just appeared at the gate. There's an ordinary wooden gate here with wire mesh. Beyond it is a short expanse, where the twenty-six guards on morning duty are standing in two adjacent files. In front of them stands a man with the rank of jamadar, holding an unsheathed sword. As the jailer walks towards them through the wooden gate, the jamadar bellows, 'Ten…shun!' The guards stamp their feet on the ground like skittish horses to indicate that they are at attention and prepared to combat any eventuality.

Walking between the two rows of guards at the slow, stately gait that suits his position, the jailer reaches the main gate. The jamadar lifts his sword in a salute, which the jailer returns by touching his forehead with his right hand. Almost immediately the gargantuan iron gates of the jail are opened with a rumble, letting in the lord and master of the jail. Bireshwar Mukherjee, jailer.

This enormous gate is not for everyone to use. A small door next to it is meant for others. Those who enter or exit through it must stoop like cavemen. But it's different when it comes to jailer-shaheb. Having to lower his head to enter his own kingdom is not worthy of the supreme.

Opposite the iron gate is a wooden one of the same dimensions. Between the two is a paved courtyard. To its left is the jailer's office. The jailer pauses on the flight of steps leading to it, while the two rows of guards march off. They will now take up their positions in different parts of the jail. The responsibility for maintaining discipline and applying the rules of the jail rests entirely on their shoulders for the next eight hours. Those who were on night duty will be relieved now.

The jailer's office is quite large, but not particularly well furnished. It appears to be in the same condition in which the British rulers had surrendered it to Indians. Not just the office but the entire jail, where none of the procedures has changed since then.

A large desk occupies the centre of the jailer's office. On it stand a small and charming model of a cannon, a tumbler, a pen-stand, an ashtray, and an idol of the goddess Kali. This last is the artistic output of a prisoner, which had been given space on the desk by a previous jailer. The present jailer does not have much faith in gods and goddesses, but he has not removed the idol. It isn't doing any harm, after all.

A hot cup of tea arrives almost as soon as he sits down. The tea has been made and brought by Shibua, a prisoner whom the jail authorities trust implicitly. From the jail office to the chauka – jail parlance for kitchen – the hospitals, the cells, the wards – he has unlimited access everywhere. No one stops him. Everyone knows that no matter what Shibua might do, escaping from jail is not the sort of misadventure he will attempt. And where will he go anyway if he escapes?

Considering that he comes to this jail twice a year without fail, what can he gain from such foolishness? On the contrary, he will lose the trust reposed in him.

After the morning headcount, he goes to the office, makes tea, lays out cups and plates, and serves the jailer, the deputy-jailer, the godown clerk, the gate warder, the security officer, and himself, after which he wanders around the jail, collecting information from its nooks and crannies.

Finishing his tea, jailer-babu signs the attendance register. Another day begins, with its attendant trial by fire. That's the right expression. Fires are raging both inside and outside the jail these days, and every day has to be spent swimming across this river of flames. Bireshwar Mukherjee has never had to face such difficult circumstances during his long working life.

There were many crises in the jail he was in charge of earlier. Sometimes it had felt as though the entire jail, with its thousands of prisoners, would sink in a treacherous sea like the Titanic. But Bireshwar Mukherjee's intelligence, courage, presence of mind and forthright leadership had saved the day. The prison had remained secure and emerged untouched from every crisis.

But the nature of those problems was different, completely unlike the current one. Defeated in his attempts to tackle it, Bireshwar Mukherjee's predecessor has gone on leave, with the sword of suspension hanging over his head.

'Good morning, sir.' Returning the greeting, the jailer looks up. He knows who it is even without setting eyes on the speaker. He knows deputy jailer Mohini-babu's voice well by now.

Mohinimohon Dasgupta. It is difficult to justify the name, considering he oozes none of the charm it suggests. It is hard to imagine that anyone has ever been captivated by Mohinimohon-babu, despite the valiant efforts made by his name. Less than five feet tall, he is conspicuously bald, has a pair of beady eyes and a flat nose which constantly drips with a yellow phlegm. His moustache is discoloured thanks to his habit of using snuff.

Bireshwar Mukherjee is a handsome man in comparison. Dark, over six feet tall, and a lean muscular frame.

The deputy jailer's office is further inside. After he ambles off in that direction, the jailer goes out to the wide courtyard to go on his rounds. The number of inmates is written with chalk on a blackboard on the wall opposite the entrance to his office. The capacity of the jail is about twelve hundred. But no jail can afford to stick to its capacity in current circumstances, when the youth are exploding with impatience against the system and rage against the state, and are desperate to bring about a radical change in society. There are widespread murders, violence, gunfire and bombing. Every ward is now stuffed with four or five times the number of prisoners it can actually hold.

The jailer looks away from the blackboard. Shibua, Bashudeb, Anil and two or three other prisoners are trying to suspend a giant scale from a hook in the roof. This is a daily task for them. The suppliers will soon be here with their vegetables or fish or meat. This team will weigh everything and clean it before taking delivery, after which the supplies will be despatched to the chauka for the cooking to begin.

A cart piled high with vegetables is already at the iron gate. Enough for two meals for nearly four and a half thousand people. The regular menu at the jail consists of dal and a vegetable curry. Fish is served once a week and meat, once a month.

A prisoner died in the clash between inmates and guards last month. The quality of the food caused the incident, which led the previous jailer to be subjected to the baleful glare of an enquiry. Chinre and gur were served for breakfast that morning. It was a fact that the chinre was stale – melly and a little bitter. Prisoners everywhere in the country have long been used to substandard food. Jailed criminals consume it uncomplainingly. They assume they are in jail to be punished, and one of the methods is to be made to eat third-rate food. In this jail, the grubby, rotting rice will inevitably be full of grit, white insects will float on the surface of the dal, the unpalatable dish of mixed vegetables will include sand and dirt in plentiful quantities. Several sacks of wheat will be unloaded on the cement floor of the kitchen to be kneaded by six or seven pairs of filthy feet. There's nothing to be done. One has to survive on this food. Those who refuse to eat will die either of starvation or of beatings.

But the Naxal prisoners were not willing to accept this age-old tradition. They made a huge fuss over the bitter chinre, rolling it into balls and flinging it at the jailer who was on his rounds, shouting slogans at the same time. Was this food fit for humans? This lead to a skirmish with the guards, which quickly escalated into a pitched battle, followed by the death and a divisional enquiry.

It is for all these reasons that the present jailer is particularly worried. A secure retirement awaits him, if he can only pass his remaining years on the job the way he has the previous twenty-five. He can enjoy the rest of his life on his pension, provident fund, gratuity and all the riches he has amassed over the years.

But it doesn't look likely. These insolent Naxals will not allow his working days to pass smoothly. There are fifty-two jails in Bengal, in each of which they are sparking some sort of incident every day. Many jail superintendents are getting a bad name and being suspended. 'What if something happens to me too?' No one notices, but Bireshwar Mukherjee trembles with constant fear and anxiety. An invisible crack has appeared in the impenetrable wall of his courage.

A large number of the people imprisoned in this jail are workers of different political parties. But no matter how militant they are in their own territories, in jail they are all docile and obedient. Appearing for the headcount five times a day, accepting their food three times a day, appearing in court once a fortnight, appointing a lawyer in deference of the law, trying to secure freedom through official channels, such as bail or an affidavit – they are not opposed to following any of these guidelines of prison life. But the problem is with the Naxals. Even if they agree to appear in court, they do not appoint lawyers. It seems they are in jail with the sole intention of defying and demolishing its solid walls as well as its rules and regulations.

All prisoners here are equal and independent. But independence does not amount to anarchy. The freedom given to inmates must be enjoyed in conformance with the jail system and through cooperation with the authorities. The prisoners' status or position outside jail is not under consideration here. As long as an inmate follows jail discipline, he can stay here undisturbed, without fearing the tools of punishment, such as being thrashed with sticks or belts, having chains clamped on his ankles, or being put in solitary confinement.

But there are some prisoners whose only reasons for being in jail are slitting the throats of landowners or killing policemen and grabbing their weapons, all with the aim of effecting a revolutionary transformation by grabbing state power. They have not become remotely well-behaved or less belligerent. Their objective now is to paralyse the systems and the tight security of the prison, so as to stage a jailbreak and escape. They never fail to convey this proudly to the authorities – escaping from jail is part of our revolutionary struggle.

Five prisoners have been transferred recently from another jail to this one. They have been kept in Cell No. 12, the most secure place here. They are the ones the authorities fear the most. They had planned a jailbreak earlier – what assurance did anyone have that they wouldn't do it again? Although they have been shifted from the sub-jail of a district town to Calcutta's most impregnable prison, they do not appear disheartened.

If they do manage to break out of prison, Bireshwar Mukherjee's spotless record of twenty-five years will have a bucket of black ink upended on it. The anxiety gnaws away at him every day. All will be well if only it ends well. Just a few years to go. Will they pass without incident?

This is when the jailer is reminded of the Hindi saying: Jab geedar ki maut aati hai toh woh shaher ke or bhagta hai. When death is imminent the wolf abandons the jungle for the city... He feels the same way. He used to have a happy existence as the supreme commander of a sub-jail in a district town. Supplies of fresh fish, meat and fruit, and of vegetables grown in the jail garden – all the ingredients of a comfortable and relaxed life. The problems in that jail were nowhere near as impossible to solve, nor were they caused by people as undaunted and indomitable as these. Who knows what lies in wait?

The jamadar on the shift has stationed each of the twenty-six guards at their respective positions, conducted a second headcount, and returned to the main gate. He will now play the role of companion and bodyguard to the jailer on his first round. He is accompanied by the guard Bir Bahadur. A no-nonsense man from Bihar, Bir Bahadur has unshakeable faith in both the gau mata and Bharat mata. Because of his devotion to cows, he considers Muslims his enemies. And his devotion to the country makes him want to kill communists on sight. Gandhi baba ne kitna mushkil se desh ko azaad kia. And after Gandhi's sacrifices to secure freedom for the country, yeh saale firse humein ghulam banaana chahtein hain. But we won't let them enslave us again. His rage is concentrated on Naxals. The bastards are Chinese agents. Those same Chinese who had attacked us in '62.

It's said that a Naxal was sentenced to death in the jail where Bir Bahadur was posted earlier. But it was proving difficult to carry out the sentence because an executioner could not be found. The convict was not only a Naxal but also a Muslim. Bir Bahadur had volunteered his services. Koi baat nahin, saale ko hum latka denge. But his offer to hang the convict was not accepted, because the High Court reviewed the sentence and changed it.

The jailer and his bodyguards are accompanied by two or three trusted prisoners. These people get no salary for their services, but they get favourable treatment from the authorities. For which they are ready to work four times as much as the employees here. Suppose an inmate is found to be defiantly rebellious, these people will fix him in the course of a single night. From forcing urine down his throat to making him perform fellatio, they have several weapons of torture at their disposal.

No matter how cruel and partial to torture a guard or officer is, his job forces him to operate under some limitations. He cannot be tyrannical while following the rules, unlike hardcore criminals who can act outside the law. Even though these restraints are sometimes relaxed or even ignored to some extent in certain political situations, or out of sheer indulgence, they cannot be removed altogether. This is when help is needed from such loyal prisoners. They perform the required task with great success.

The advantage is that no blame can be attached to the employees of the jail. No one can be suspended or dismissed. Human rights organizations and journalists are kept in the dark. 'The incident involved two groups of prisoners. We are investigating to find out who was responsible. Suitable action will be taken.' The situation can be managed with such assurances.

Jamadar Raghubir Tiwari is carrying a fat register, with a cane baton tucked under his arm. He is bald and bespectacled, and there are drops of milk on his moustache. A drum filled with milk arrives every day, meant for patients in the hospital. The patients get only what is left over after the milk is distributed amongst eighteen guards, three jamadars and prisoners loyal to the authorities.

Raghubir has extracted his due. His moustache holds the evidence.

The jailer smiles at Raghubir without saying a word. That would be inappropriate, beyond the bounds of decency. As everyone knows, if you fancy having an elephant in your yard, it's no use mourning for the trees it will eat. Bireshwar Mukherjee begins his rounds slowly.

The guard on duty unlocks the large wooden gates. Outside the iron gates is the free world of free people. Two guards take up position alertly on either side of this gate whenever it's unlocked, not allowing any of the prisoners to come close. But there is no need to observe so much caution when unlocking the wooden gate. It is a prisoner who pushes it open.

Beyond this gate is a green field, at the far end of which stands the watchtower, set against the high wall. The inmates used to play football here earlier. This has been stopped for reasons of security. Unlike the other walls, there is no ten-foot-high iron railing in front of this one, which makes it relatively vulnerable. That is why the movement of prisoners here is restricted.

The jailer walks eastward along the path bordering the field. He is followed by the jamadar, who leads the entourage.

Ahead and left lies the case-table. This is the internal courtroom of the jail. It has nothing to do with the crimes committed by the prisoners outside. This is for judging crimes committed inside the jail. Someone may have been found with a razor-blade or some marijuana, someone else may have fought with other inmates or been caught in a homosexual act – there are arrangements for suitable punishment based on the gravity of the crime. Among these are suspending the wrongdoer by handcuffs from a railing for five or six hours; clamping chains around their ankles to prevent them from moving about, sitting, or lying down comfortably; placing them in solitary confinement for a week or ten days.

As the prisoners put it: there's a jail inside the jail, its name is the cell. Spending a month or two in these five feet by seven feet compartments with no light or fresh air is bound to break any prisoner. But there are exceptions. Who knows what life force it is that enables Naxals to spend years inside those cells without their spirits being killed? They laugh loudly, they talk, they sing, some of them even write poetry. This is an extraordinary affair.

The ward by the case-table, facing the field next door, is called Amdani. All new imports brought to the jail from the courtroom spend their first nights here. About thirty such fresh prisoners are now squatting on their haunches in pairs outside amdani. The jamadar will assign them to different wards after the jailer has completed his round.

Six cells are situated adjacent to amdani. A high wall surrounds the cells, with an iron gate leading into them. The guard here is always on high alert. The cells are currently occupied by five Naxals found guilty of heinous crimes. They have conspired and declared war against the state. The jailer walks on eastward, looking around him. Wards on either side, each surrounded by high iron railings at a little distance from the buildings. A twenty-foot wide unpaved road runs between the railings. It could easily have been paved with bricks, but what if the prisoners were to rip the bricks up and use them as weapons?

The two-storied buildings on either side have been divided into separate numbered wards. There are twenty-four wards in all. Ward No. 7 on the ground floor of the building on the left is reserved for Naxals. It has fifty-six occupants.

The path between the wards ends at another ten-foot-high iron railing, on the other side of which runs the same high wall, with a watchtower looming over it. An alert sentry mans the tower, his finger always poised on the trigger. If a prisoner clambers over the iron railing and approaches the wall, he will fire at once – that is the rule.

Another path wends northward from this spot. Next to it stands the enormous kitchen. The dal, vegetables and rice are cooked here in a dozen gigantic vessels, each placed on a huge earthen stove. Fifty or so prisoners have begun cooking for the day. The boiled peas meant for breakfast have already been despatched to the wards.

Having inspected the kitchen, the jailer walks on. Now the path turns to the west. The hospital is situated a little further down. Next to it is a small lunatic asylum. A mad man locked in there bursts into laughter at the sight of the jailer, and then breaks into foul language. The jailer knows that although the guard on duty at the hospital isn't reacting now, the lunatic will be beaten up mercilessly for his invectives.

The jailer doesn't spend too much time at the hospital, entering through one gate and exiting through another. The hospital is empty now. It is being cleaned. The doctor hasn't arrived yet. He will be here at ten.

The doctor is known as Pagla Daktar, the mad doctor, in jail. He cannot stand thieves, robbers and pickpockets. And if it's someone convicted of rape, he flares up in rage at the very sight of the person. Sometimes he even snatches the stick from a guard and lands a couple of blows on the convict. But despite all this the man is honest. No one has succeeded in accusing him of corruption. Normally, the supply of essential lifesaving drugs to jail hospitals is minimal. Still, he uses whatever little he gets strictly for patients. When he has a cup of tea at the hospital, it's made with tea leaves he has bought outside with his own money. While others sip tea with milk that isn't watered down, he drinks nothing but black tea.

But just like the one proverbial bad apple that spoils the crop, all his qualities are eclipsed by one little flaw. He is sympathetic towards Naxal prisoners, a fact that he makes no attempt to hide, declaring openly, 'They're not criminals, for heaven's sake. All of them well-educated boys from decent families. Decent families. Does a single mistake mean they've become animals now?'

Thanks to his sympathy, anyone who falls ill in the cells or in Ward No. 7 does not have to visit the doctor; it's the doctor who visits the patient. 'Ei Bijon, why are your eyes red? Come here...' The doctor drops by twice every day to check on everyone's health.

The jailer would not have been able to leave so early if the doctor had been there, for that would have meant a conversation. Bireshwar Mukherjee has run into all kinds of people in jails. There's been no dearth of mad men among them, but he's encountering a mad doctor for the first time. Nor has he met such a workaholic government employee before. It is normal to have the working day defined by the clock, but here is someone who doesn't care how many hours he spends working, be it day or night. Who else but a mad man will behave this way?

After the hospital, the jailer turns to the south. This path leads back to the case-table. On the way, he stops abruptly at the door to the cells. Chhotelal, the guard on duty here, swiftly hides the cup of tea with the unadulterated milk that is his due and snaps to attention. Five faces belonging to five prisoners can be seen behind the thick iron gate. They have just started their hour of freedom outside their cells after being locked inside them for twelve hours. They will use this hour to clear their bowels and have their breakfast before trooping back into their cells. They will be released again for an hour before noon for a bath and lunch, and then for a couple of hours between four and six in the evening. They remain locked inside their cells during the remaining twenty hours every day.

The five of them are pacing up and down in the corridor outside the cells now, chatting and laughing amongst themselves. They don't seem to be afflicted in any way in mind, body or spirit. In fact, they are in a constant state of unbelievably heightened excitement.

Stopping in his tracks, the jailer spots five pairs of eyes trained on him through the gaps in the bolted iron gates like powerful flashlights, whose beams seem to transmit mockery, amusement and contempt.

Bireshwar Mukherjee comes to a quick decision. He's not going to bow before them or reveal any sort of vulnerability. It's a war of nerves. A display of anxiety will provide extra ammunition to his opponents. It will be foolish to allow this. It is essential that they understand how capable the state and its security forces are, and that this strength is multiplied further when it comes to prisons.

He knows how much power the state has put in his hands so that he can maintain peace, regulations and discipline in this walled zone which is cut off from the rest of the world. Then why should he weaken?...

How short and yet how deadly the names were: Little Boy and Fat Man. They had caused the deaths of hundreds of thousands in an instant. There's an equally beautiful and melodious codeword used in jails: pagla-ghanti. The incessant clanging of a huge bell. Those who have never been inside a jail do not know that the pagla-ghanti is in fact the official announcement of a hellish ritual of human slaughter. Even the boldest prisoner's blood runs cold at the mention of the pagla-ghanti.

The moment a guard on duty in a jail senses anything abnormal or out of place, or a potential breach of security, he is supposed to blow the whistle in his pocket. Any other guard who hears it is also supposed to start blowing his own whistle. From one guard to another, the sound will be relayed to the main gate, where the guard on duty must immediately start ringing the large brass bell hanging over there. The clanging of the bell will be joined by the wail of the siren, very similar to air-raid alarms in wartime. The siren rises to a crescendo and then drops to a low note before climbing again. Amidst these peaks and troughs of the siren, accompanied by the clanging of the bell, the guards' barracks will spring into action. No matter where they are or what they are doing, they are supposed to dash towards the main gate of the jail with their sticks. Never mind if someone is barely dressed for he has been in the bathroom, or if someone has flour dough on their hand for he has been busy making his dinner. Someone may have been in the arms of his wife or a woman not his wife, he too will gather at the gate, lipstick stains and all. The main gates will be opened with a rumble. All of them will rush in. The jamadar on duty will be leading them with an unsheathed sword. If it's dark there will be flaming torches everywhere. At the same time, armed sentries from a battalion stationed next door will surround the jail on all sides. One group will follow the guards into the jail. If the stick-wielding guards do not achieve the desired results the sentries will step in. The constant ringing of the pagla-ghanti is a simple message: 'No restraint needs to be maintained'. Once this message has reached everyone, there remains just the one instruction to come from the jailer: 'Act as you please now.'

At once the guards will pounce on the prisoners like mad dogs. They will use their five-foot-long sticks, which are no less than clubs, to attack the inmates on their heads, chests, stomachs, backs, hips, knees – anywhere they like, as mercilessly as they want. Skulls will be split and grey matter will be splattered on the walls, the floor will be afloat in blood, an apocalypse will be heard in the shrieks and screams of countless injured people.

Let it be heard. No one will witness what goes on inside this walled universe, out of sight of people. It's enough to dispose of the corpses under cover of the night in a black van, and to rinse off the bloodstains. All that remains is the discrepancy in the headcount, which can be easily explained as a successful escape on the part of the dead men.

No authority with such absolute power at his disposal can possibly betray weakness. Even if he has any, it must not be seen.

Going up to the door leading into the cell, the jailer instructs the guard tersely, 'Unlock the gate.' Surprised, the guard complies. Bireshwar Mukherjee approaches the five young men in the corridor. 'I've come to meet you. I hope this unannounced visit is not a problem.'

The five of them come to a halt. Porimal, tall, fair and with a face like a poet's, says with a smile, 'This is your kingdom. You can come and go as you please.'

'That is true. But your response will help me decide whether to visit you again or not.'

Porimal smiles again. 'You're the full-time head of this jail. Visiting the cells is part of your duty. It's natural for a prisoner not to be elated by proximity to the jailer. But in the course of our long years in prison, we have come across many people whose sensitivities have not been killed by the work they do. It will be a pleasure for us if you're one of them.'

After a pause the jailer says, 'You can trust me when I say that I will not be unduly harsh with you. I won't hesitate to give you all the benefits allowed by the rules and regulations of the jail. But you will also have to promise you will not misuse these benefits.'

Bireshwar Mukherjee was a schoolteacher before joining the jail service. He continues declaiming like a lecturer in class, 'The immense landmass from Kashmir to Kanyakumari whose name is India has its own culture of creativity, literature and art. Some ten million military and civil defenders are perpetually prepared to protect its independence, sovereignty and integrity. To declare war against such a country or such a force with a dozen bombs or homemade guns is not the sign of a mature mentality. Whoever it is who has deluded you will certainly repent eventually. I try to appreciate your situation not in terms of the law but with my heart. I don't want you to do anything that will cause you irreparable harm.'

'We have studied this extensively,' says Porimal. 'We have visited the interiors of India to understand the causes of the widespread oppression, deprivation, poverty and malnutrition. We have come to the conclusion that the disease cannot be cured without surgery. Everything has to be dismantled and rebuilt. Complete change, in other words. You can call it delusion or aberration or immaturity. We realise that when a person speaks, when he presents an argument or an analysis, it isn't just the person alone who is speaking, but also his earlier history, class, family, blood-group, economic and social status, education and experience. What you just said is not just your personal viewpoint, you represent an entire class. We don't share this view. That leaves the power of the state. We all know that the state wields unlimited power. But whom does this power depend on? The police, the military – who are they? All of them have been born into starving and penniless families of peasants. Is it possible that they never think of their own past, of their families, of other impoverished and subjugated people? That would turn history into a lie. All equations will change the day they turn around. They're bound to change. And what was that you were talking of...oh yes, you were talking of harm. Harm to us. Thank you for your advice. It's just that we know that in order to ensure freedom for millions, it might be necessary for thousands, or even hundreds of thousands, to become cripples, to rot in jail, even to be hanged or shot. The ruling classes do not give up power voluntarily. There is no example of any tyrant abdicating without using all the power at his disposal. Therefore we may indeed come to grave harm. Assuming you consider losing one's life harmful. If such a situation does arise, we won't retreat, you'll see. We have had two paglis here, two jailbreak situations. No one died in the first, but many of us had to spend a long time in the hospital afterwards. Two of us were martyred in the second.

We hope we've been able to prove on both occasions that we won't cow down.'

Beads of sweat have appeared on Porimal's brow after this long speech. He is a little worked up. 'All right, all right,' says the jailer. 'You must do what you think is best. Who will prevent you? And why will you allow them to? But I give you my guarantee that I won't make any pre-emptive moves. As a gesture of goodwill, you no longer need to go back into lock-up at eight in the morning. Let me know if you face any other problems.'

'Why don't you say something?' Porimal tells Bijon, who's standing next to him.

Bijon is an extremely fair, extremely thin twenty-two-year-old.

'We don't have any particular problem,' he says a trifle sarcastically. 'We're quite well. As well as can be in a jail, that is. We don't need any other benefits. But a right that was given to us under court orders is being denied us right now.'

'What! Please explain.'

'We pay for a newspaper to be delivered to us. It is not through secret channels, nor is it published by our own organization. Still we find that some news items are being cut out of the newspaper before it reaches us. This is completely illegal. We hope you will look into this.'

Bireshwar Mukherjee shrugs off the sarcasm. 'I've asked for this,' he says, 'keeping in mind your mental state. Personally I feel it would be best if you stopped reading these newspapers. Why bother? It just creates unnecessary pressure. I've seen your case files. I think you'll be sentenced to twenty...yes, twenty years. Mankind is making so much progress in the fields of science and arts and health and education. The nation is marching ahead. While all of you are rotting in dark cells. Anyone will be depressed in this situation. So...'

'Are you certain things will turn out as you just predicted?'

'What things?'

'That we'll rot in jail for twenty years.'

'Or you might be hanged.'

Suddenly a dark young man with large eyes, whose name is Nemai, says from the back of the group, 'Or we could be free in a day or two.'

'How?'

'We know how, and it's not as though you don't know either.'

'You'll escape?'

'That's not a question which can be answered.'

'Why not?'

Porimal, who is probably their ideological leader, says, 'Look, the jail is a symbol of the conceit and arrogance of the state apparatus. It pats itself on the back every time it puts a revolutionary behind bars. It considers itself secure. The imprisoned revolutionary's duty is to destroy this arrogance. In the process, he tears down not just the walls of the jail but also the determination of the ruling class. He proves that no fortress of the administration is impregnable. Therefore, breaking out of jail is part of our strategy. We will never give you our word not to attempt a jailbreak. Even if anyone promises as much, they won't keep it.'

'Hmm,' says the jailer. He's got an impression of the resoluteness of the prisoners in the cells. Suitable action will have to be taken. But something rankles him. A sensation of defeat... How can they be so steadfast in their cause?

He then continues on his way. There's no point lingering here.

He feels five pairs of eyes boring into his back.

TWO

The jailer goes on his first round at 6 AM, the second at 11 AM, and the last at 6 PM. Of course, he can take as many more rounds as he likes in between. It all depends on the situation at hand. But Bireshwar Mukherjee does not limit himself to the three routine rounds, he also walks around at the three mealtimes, observing closely. His predecessor had got into trouble over food – he is alert to the possibility of a recurrence and intends to prevent it.

Normally the grains and vegetables supplied to the jail are not of very high quality. Besides, their quantity is far lower than stipulated. Then there is widespread pilferage down the line, starting at the very top. This organised theft is impossible to stop officially. Attempting this will have the jailer dismissed by his own boss in the government. But Bireshwar Mukherjee does try to ensure that there is no large-scale theft of whatever reaches the godowns, that it gets to the people it is meant for. He has to ignore small things like someone on the staff making a cup of tea with milk meant for patients. He gets his tea too the same way. He has to guard against entire sacks of food being spirited away. Preventing theft in any jail is a difficult task. Who will police the policemen? All the guards are infected to some extent. If the guard on duty at the gate today searches the bag of the guard who is returning to the barracks after his shift and confiscates stolen material, the favour is bound to be returned when the roles are reversed tomorrow. There will be revenge. Far better to live on the frictionless fraternal relationship of steal and let steal.

The quantity of rice in the rations has been reduced recently under government orders. The prisoners can no longer be served more than 72 grams of rice for lunch. Since this isn't enough, the prisoners crowd around the drain where the starch is thrown away after the rice is made. But there isn't enough of that to go around either. Fights break out every day. A most tragic incident took place a few days ago. Lunch consists of dal, vegetables, rice and some mashed potato, which is known as aluchokha. A dozen prisoners are usually taken from the wards to the chauka to peel boiled potatoes for the aluchokha – they get eight bidis each in exchange for this voluntary labour.

Bidis are extremely precious in the jail, even working as a substitute for money sometimes. Prisoners addicted to smoking actually go so far as to sell their clothes and slippers for bidis. Many inmates offer their labour at the kitchen, at the hospital, and elsewhere in exchange for bidis. In jail parlance, each of them is known as a Faltu.

That day the prisoner who was to peel the mashed potato was starving. Unable to control himself at the sight of the food, he had picked up a potato to eat it. Everyone does this whenever they get the chance. Knowing this, the guard on duty at the kitchen always keeps an eye on the faltus and is quick to deliver a blow or two on their back when they catch them out. This faltu got his timing wrong. Even before he could take a proper bite, he saw the guard running up to him. Afraid of punishment, he tried to swallow the entire potato, but it stuck in his gullet, almost choking him to death.

It is beyond the jailer's powers to solve the problem of hunger. But Bireshwar Mukherjee does try to ensure equitable distribution of whatever is actually available. It is not just the guards but also a group of long-serving prisoners who collect much more than their due. The jailer keeps a strict watch to prevent such practices.

It's easy for prisoners and guards to be directly involved in pilferage. For they officially manage the resources of the jail. And not giving in to temptation might be difficult. But had he not seen it for himself, Bireshwar Mukherjee would never have believed that the sentries of the battalions – who do not even move about within the jail, who go directly from their barracks to the watchtowers and then back to the barracks – could still be involved in trafficking stolen goods even from that distance and height. With these sentries involved, there was no need for anyone else to risk smuggling anything out of the jail themselves.

The incident took place in the last jail Bireshwar Mukherjee had served in. One of the sentries always used to turn up for watchtower duty with a length of rope. From the tower he would drop one end of the rope inside the jail, to which a guard would attach sacks of rice and dal. The sentry would then haul it back up into the tower, and share the spoils with the guard afterwards.

Bireshwar Mukherjee had caught them himself. What happened after that is best not recounted here.

During his third round today, the jailer is astonished by something he spots in the chauka. Not just astonished but also enraged. He sees luchis – a delicacy far removed from the coarse rotis that the jail is used to – being fried with great care. Four of them are arranged on a plate already. No prisoner here is entitled to such a lavish meal. For whom are they being made, then? Moreover, frying the luchis clearly involves using resources meant for prisoners. That is a crime.

The jailer has found out from sources that luchi and alubhaja are made for the guards on morning duty every day. This is done after he has been on his rounds, which means it is unlikely, if not entirely imposssible, that he will find out. News of his leaving his office to carry out inspections is usually relayed instantly to the kitchen, so that they can hide the evidence before he gets there. But observing a prisoner frying luchis with such great concentration despite his presence naturally makes him furious. How dare a thief be so audacious! 'What's going on?' he demands sternly. 'What's all this?' Turning the luchi over to fry the other side, the prisoner answers, 'Onar aajker diet. This is what he'll eat today.'

'He! Who's this he?'

Jamadar Bindeshwari Dubey is standing nearby. For some unknown reason, he steps forward to shield the prisoner. 'You don't know, sir? Hasn't anyone told you about him? All this is for nobody but him.'

The jailer is perplexed. Who is this 'him'? There's no prisoner of exalted status in this jail. Nor anyone awaiting execution. The only inmates are prisoners under trial for theft and robbery, and those Naxals. For which great personage is this royal repast meant, then – someone whom even the jamadar is in awe of?

Senior Jamadar Bindeshwari Dubey is a leader in the structure of jail security. Everyone respects him. But for a guard to revere a prisoner is very abnormal...

If all this is meant for a prisoner, it must be someone very important. And yet the jailer is not aware of him, doesn't know his name, hasn't even met him. This amounts to negligence on the jailer's part. Turning to the jamadar, Bireshwar Mukherjee rasps, 'Jamadar-babu, I don't want any coded messages. Tell me clearly what all this is about. Who is it for? Here we have people fighting one another for scraps while someone else is having a feast. This is not right. All of you seem to know... I'm the only one in the dark. Tell me at once, who is it?'

'You've been here a month, sir,' the jamadar says defensively. 'I assumed you had come to know by now. Abhi malum hua aap unke baare mein kuch nahi jante. Now that I know you haven't been told, I'll tell you everything, let's go to your office.'

'What's the problem with telling me here?'

'It's a long story, sir. It will take time...'

'For now all I need to know is whom this is for. Is it a prisoner or a guard?'

'A prisoner, sir.'

'What's his name? Which ward?'

'He doesn't belong to a ward anymore, sir. Used to be in No. 1. Now you can consider him as living all over the jail. Kabhi idhar toh kabhi udhar.'

Is this really the senior jamadar speaking, the man who is in charge of the seventy-two guards here, who is a shareholder in the fate of the jail, for good or for bad? Is he really telling a senior officer that there is a prisoner who is not locked up, who is not included in the headcount, whose whereabouts inside the jail no one is sure of? Doesn't he know the trouble he can get into for making such a foolish statement?

'Do you know what you're saying?' the jailer asks. 'What if this prisoner who roams around at will escapes from jail?'

'He won't escape,' the jamadar answers with self-assurance. 'He's been here since 1962. Without escaping. It would be best for everyone if he escaped, but he refuses to...'

'Best if he escaped!' The jailer is shocked. 'How will you match the headcount?'

'He's no longer part of the headcount. He's beyond all headcounts. You'll understand once I explain.'

'So why don't you explain right now?' the jailer asks impatiently. 'Why all this secrecy about a prisoner? I need to know everything. What is his name?'

'He did have a name once, but now he's known as Bandiswala.'

'Bandiswala!'

'Ji saab. He's wrapped in bandages from head to toe, which is why everyone calls him by this name.'

The jailer is at his wits' end. He can make no sense of what he's hearing. Why bandages all over? Are the prisoner's bones and ribs fractured? There is indeed a patient in the hospital who's all bandaged up. A third degree interrogation at Lalbazar led to a broken hip. But he cannot move about, he is confined to his bed. This one, however, can be found any and everywhere. How strange!

'His entire body, from head to toe, was burnt, you see,' the senior jamadar continues. 'That's why he was wrapped up in bandages. And he has stayed that way.'

The jailer is unwilling to indulge this nonsense anymore. 'Whatever his story might be, locate him at once and lock him up. One man will be the cause of many people losing their jobs. He must not be allowed to roam free in any circumstances.'

After a short silence, the jamadar expresses his inability to comply. 'How can that be possible, sir? All the rules and regulations of the jail are for living people. But he is beyond these rules now.'

'Are you telling me he's a ghost?'

'Yes, sir. He died in 1962. But his soul is still in this jail. Many people have seen him. So will you, if you're lucky.'

'So all that special food is for this ghost.'

'Ji saab.'

Bireshwar Mukherjee is about to lose his temper with the jamadar. What does this man take him for? Is he an imbecile who thinks he can make up a cock-and-bull story to fool him? But he does not say anything. He's still a newcomer here. There's nothing to be gained by annoying his colleagues. It's obvious that someone is playing a hoax as this Bandiswala to get himself a good meal every day. But who is it? The jailer decides not to take anyone to task till he identifies this person who has the backing of the prisoners as well as guards.

There's meat for lunch at the jail today. What they actually get is the curry, which might with great difficulty yield a little minced meat. But a living human and a spirit who has transcended rules and regulations are not the same thing. The jailer observes a prisoner laying out nine or ten luchis and a bowl of specially prepared mutton on a plate.

There is a mid-sized pond in the middle of the jail. It has an abundant supply of tilapia fish. The water is green with algae. The kitchen stands to the east of this pond, and opposite the kitchen are the cells. The hospital is to the right, facing which is Ward No. 2.

A large banyan tree stands next to the kitchen on the edge of the pond. A circular platform has been erected around its base. Someone had established a Shiva Linga here. Some people pluck flowers from the jail garden and leave them here with a muttered prayer. 'Please take care of my case, o Lord. Make sure I don't get life imprisonment. Save me.'

Now one of the prisoners brings the plate of luchi and mutton and puts it down on the platform with the Shiva Linga, making sure to cover the food. He bows his head in devotion, as though offering the food to a god. Bireshwar Mukherjee no longer thinks it necessary to remain there. Before he can reach his office via the hospital, the cells and the case-table, the siren goes off. Usually this does not happen till he's finished his morning tea, but today he's been delayed by a conversation with Pagla Daktar. 'There's no such thing as ghosts, jailer-babu,' the doctor told him. 'No such thing. All bogus, nothing but bogus. They eat it themselves, putting up the ghost as a front. Those guards at the wards – they eat it. You don't know what they're like. They can eat anything. That tub of lard, what's his name, gets kitchen duty quite often. He, quite frankly, he's a camel. A camel. Apparently camels drink water once a week. And that pumpkin – my hands are tied, or I would have pronounced him unfit a long time ago. Unfit a long time ago. A prison guard with a paunch like a football. They're the ones who eat it. I can swear on it. This is a ploy. Someone died seven or eight years ago – what other reason would they have to keep him alive? They have something to gain from it. I can guarantee there are no ghosts here. No ghosts here. All bogus.'

The jailer has been told that the mad doctor injects himself with narcotics. Immediately after which he has to have a cup of strong black tea with fifty grams of sugar added. It's true he was drinking black tea when talking to the jailer. But it wasn't clear whether he had taken an injection. Still, what he had said made sense.

Seeing the deputy jailer standing before him, the jailer asks, 'Do you believe in ghosts? Do you think this story about the bandaged ghost in the jail is true?'

The deputy jailer has nothing to attend to right now. He is delighted that he can pass an hour discussing this. Taking a pinch of snuff and wiping his nose with his handkerchief, he says, 'There is enough and more evidence of this in our shastro.

Anyone who has an unnatural death, especially on a Tuesday or a Saturday, does not find release for his soul. He turns into a spirit. His incorporeal soul wanders around the site of his death for twelve years, harming living beings...'

'So you're saying the bandaged ghost exists.'

'He does. I have proof. Now that you're here, you'll have it too. He died eight years ago. If the scriptures are right, and there is no reason for them not to be, for no lie can survive thousands of years – if the scriptures are right, he will plague us another four years. Only after twelve years are completed will his soul find release.'

'But the doctor was saying there's no such thing as ghosts...'

'Forget what the mad doctor says. The soul exists and this is the inevitable outcome if it is not released from the body in a natural way.'

'But many scientists and knowledgeable people say there's no such thing as a soul. Everything ends with death.'

'Ignorant fools and godless communists say such things. I don't consider them educated. Having a degree does not amount to education. What is their rationale for claiming the soul does not exist? Distorted reasoning. If you read Swami Abhedananda's Edge of Death, you'll see he's cited not just one or two incidents but hundreds of them, all of them with names and places. And they all prove that the soul is immortal. Our own Gita says the same thing – fire cannot burn it, air cannot shrivel it, weapons cannot kill it. The soul doesn't die. Just as a human sheds one set of garments to don another, so too does a soul shed one body to take refuge in another.'

Laughing to himself, the jailer says, 'Let's say you're right. But the doctor was saying that souls, if souls do exist, they're more powerful than the living, in which case all the Naxals who have been killed by the police till now, their souls should have smashed all the jails and police stations into smithereens. What do you think about that?'

The deputy jailer lapses into a sulky silence. Then he says, 'The doctor is right. The ghosts of Naxals could certainly have done it. But do you know why they can't? Because all communists are atheists.'

'Don't communists turn into ghosts?'

'Hear me out. They're atheists, they don't believe in destiny or god or rebirth. But their families do – their parents and brothers and sisters do. So what do relatives do when they hear that their son or brother or nephew has died? They take the body to the crematorium. There they observe all the rituals and burn the body. Then they also perform all the post-death rituals. So the soul is released. Those who do not get this opportunity keep coming back even after death to satisfy all their unfulfilled desires.'

This time the jailer laughs out loudly. 'So what it amounts to is that the bandaged ghost has not found release because the rituals weren't conducted. No sraddho or anything.'

'Precisely,' answers the deputy jailer. 'He came to Calcutta from some village in Bihar. Got involved with criminals while doing different jobs like pulling rickshaws and carts and working for contractors. Then he got caught and ended up in jail. We wrote to his village address after his death. No one turned up to claim the corpse. Who knows whether the address was right? When they're caught, thieves give false names not just for themselves but even for their fathers. As for addresses…'

Blowing his nose, the deputy jailer says, 'Want to hear a story?'

'Is it a story or an actual incident?'

'An incident. But because I heard about it from others, I call it a story. Once, a pickpocket was caught. He'd barely slipped his hand into someone's pocket, not even managed to steal anything yet. IPC 397. Ninety days in jail at the outside. At the police station, he said his name was Biren Datta, and his father's name, Naren Datta. Which of course is Swami Vivekananda's name. On the day of his release though, he simply couldn't remember his father's name. He'd made up a name when he was caught three months ago, and hadn't had to use it since. So obviously he'd forgotten. But no one can be released from jail unless they get their father's name right. He was tearing his hair out in frustration. Suddenly he remembered he'd used the name of a holy man he'd met at a jatra performance for Ramkrishna Paramhansa. So when the deputy jailer asked, what's your father's name, he nonchalantly said, Vivekananda Datta. The deputy jailer lost his temper and said, you said Naren last time, you bastard, and now you're saying Vivekananda. The pickpocket realised he'd made a mistake. So he said, he was young then, so I mentioned the name he had in his youth. Now he's much older, so I'm telling you the name he uses now. The deputy jailer was perplexed. How could anyone become much older in three months? Undaunted, the pickpocket said, you don't know my father. If you'd watched the ramkeshto jatra, you'd have known how much older he got in just three hours, never mind three months.'

The jailer bursts into laughter. 'Marvellous story, true or not. Never mind that, tell me about this bandage affair. How do we tackle this? This luchi-manghsho business doesn't look right.'

'There's nothing to be done. Let things go on the same way for four years more. It's either that or organising a proper set of rituals for him – hom-joggo-sraddho-shanti.' The deputy jailer sounds aggrieved. 'My gurudeb from Haridwar was here recently. We could have done it all quite cheaply. Mr Sanyal, you know the earlier jailer was called Sanyal-babu, don't you, went to missionary schools, brought up in a Western way. Made great strides at an early age. He refused to accept what I was saying. I don't believe in any of this, he said. And besides, if there really is a bandage-wrapped ghost in the jail, why not let him remain? He's not harming anyone. He just wanders about – and removes his bandage for a close look at anyone he suspects of being a casewala. Let him feast his eyes, what's the problem? We'd have got rid of the ghost a long time ago if Sanyal-babu had given his permission. We wouldn't have had to spend a penny. The vegetable and fish-suppliers were ready to pay for everything.'

Casewalas are prisoners charged with the same crime. But why does Bandiswala seek out casewalas?

'It was his casewala who murdered him. That's what makes him look for his murderer. He's perpetually seeking revenge. Which is all very well, but consider this: people do resemble one another, don't they? When filmstars use body doubles, can you tell them apart? What if there's someone here who looks like his casewala? Who will save the man? Think about it: if someone in a ward or a cell were to be found throttled to death, wouldn't the responsibility be ours? What excuse will we give then? How will we save our jobs?'

'That's easy, we'll just say a ghost did it.'

'Saying won't be enough. They'll want proof.'

'We'll provide proof. Criminology says there's no such thing as a perfect murder. The murderer always leaves a clue. That will enable us to identify the killer.'

'In my opinion, prevention is better than cure,' says the deputy jailer.

'What do you suggest then? A religious ritual?'

'If you consider it suitable. What more can I say? My gurudeb will be visiting Tarapith next month. If you like, I can...'

'Let me think about it. Since there's a problem, there has to be a solution.'

THREE

Having worked like a dog all day in the kitchen, Navalkishore should have been fast asleep in the corridor of Ward No. 5, like he used to every other night. But he was simply unable to sleep. Anxiety is the arch-enemy of slumber. Sleep had been eluding him for the past few days. After seven years of imprisonment, the deputy jailer had informed him that he would be free in just ten days. Ever since then sleep had deserted his eyes. Why was he not overjoyed at the prospect of this long-sought freedom? On the contrary, his chest was heavy with a dull, recurrent pain. This was not at the thought of separation from his companions of all these years. Its origin lay in the fact that his casewala Lachman Singh, his fellow convict for the same crime as his, would be freed four days before him. Navalkishore was overcome with grief and panic at this. If only I could have been released four days earlier, or his release delayed by four days!

They had entered the jail together, having been given identical sentences for the crime they had committed together. They should have been released on the same day too. But a poisonous snake had upset all calculations. A snake that had bitten Navalkishore to ensure that while he would not die, he would suffer from the venom all his life.

No one knew how the snake had got in. Perhaps it had slithered in through the sewage drain and then hidden itself in the flower garden to grow stronger. Lachman Singh had happened to catch sight of it on his way back from delivering the food at the amdani ward. The food was usually carried in a vat slung from a bamboo stick. Lachman Singh had used this bamboo stick at once to crush the head of the snake. As a reward for this act of courage, his sentence was remitted by four days.

All prisoners can have their sentences reduced this way in return for useful acts like these. The superintendent can reduce the sentence by a month, the jailer by a week, and the senior jamadar by a day. Killing a poisonous snake falls into this category of acts. But despite turning the jail upside down, Navalkishore could not find a snake to kill. And so he was lagging four days behind Lachman Singh when it came to being released.

Four days. A very long time. Navalkishore could not bear the agony. A man could reach the moon in four days. Lachman Singh could go away to any corner of the world in four days, making it impossible to find him.

Seven years had passed in jail. Navalkishore had not suffered for even a day. All he had told himself was that once these seven years had passed, he could spend the rest of his life in affluence. But those hopes were dashed now. There was no doubt that with four days' head start, Lachman Singh would collect the gold biscuits they had buried together and disappear. Navalkishore had often fantasized about being released a bare half an hour before Lachman Singh. He would grab the entire loot himself and vanish in Nepal. Surely Lachman Singh had the same idea.

That was the way things worked in this field. Anyone who could betray a partner would do it. Considering friends could slit each other's throats for a thousand rupees or two, this was a king's ransom.

The two of them had robbed the famous jeweller Aditya Chowdhury's shop together. It was an outrageous crime. Just two people carrying out a heist in broad daylight.

The shop had two businesses running out of it, one openly and the other in secret. The first was the same as that of every other jewellery shop. The second one involved gold biscuits smuggled in via boats, which were used to make ornaments and then sold clandestinely.

This secret business was obviously not legal, which was why no accounts were maintained for general consumption. So Aditya Chowdhury could not disclose to anyone just how big his loss from the robbery was. Navalkishore and Lachman Singh had buried the loot at a spot marked with a sign that only the two of them could identify. The idea was to dig it up later. But before that they were caught selling gold ornaments they had stolen earlier and sentenced to jail.

Obviously, the first one to be released would hit the jackpot. And this was giving Navalkishore sleepless nights.

Risking his life for the robbery, followed by a fortnight of third degree torture in the police station, and then seven years of being grilled by the heat of the ovens in the chauka – all wasted. What was he to do? There was just one option: prevent Lachman Singh from getting out. In any way possible. By killing him if necessary. If he could twist a gamchha around Lachman Singh's throat and tighten the noose, the outcome would be what was known in jail parlance as khallaas. Of course, there was the risk of being caught. So the murder had to be carried out in a way that would make it look like an accident.

The night passed plotting the murder. Finally the sun rose. The jail woke up to cries of 'File! File!' from the guards. All the prisoners squatted in pairs, rubbing the sleep out of their eyes. A jamadar and his bodyguard conducted the headcount, noting the numbers in their record books. After the numbers were tallied, the siren rang out. The ward gates were opened. The prisoners moved into the open spaces in front of the buildings. They would have their breakfast, defecate, and return to the wards.

Those who had to put in labour at the kitchen or godown or elsewhere headed off to work. There would be a second headcount at the respective workplaces. No wonder the prisoners had a rhyme: Kam khana jaada gona uska naam jailkhana. Count their heads don't give them food, that's what makes a jail so good.

After the first headcount, Navalkishore and Lachman Singh were both in the kitchen now. Today's menu was lopsi, a watery gruel. Their job was to deliver the food to the wards.

Those who would cook the gruel were at work already lighting the ovens.

There was no time. Navalkishore had to act right now. The next time gruel was to be served would be a week later, by which time Lachman Singh would have flown the coop. He could not be given that opportunity. As the gruel was made, Navalkishore prepared himself. Lachman Singh was a carefree man that day, he looked positively cheerful. He must have been delighted with his imminent release.

As soon as the giant vat of gruel was lowered from the oven, Navalkishore slotted in a thick pole of bamboo through the large rings on its side. Now it was time to hoist the pole on their shoulders, with the vat hanging from it, and deliver the food to the first floor of Ward No. 2. It was a steep staircase. Each iron vat contained enough gruel for at least a thousand people. Only the very strong could carry this weight.

'Chalein? Shall we go?' Navalkishore asked Lachman Singh.

'Yes, let's,' Lachman Singh replied. They lifted the pole on to their shoulders, but there was a change in routine today. It was Navalkishore who picked up the front end, unlike their usual practice. He had done this after a lot of calculation. They started walking towards the first floor of Ward No. 2. Lachman Singh, carrying the rear end of the pole, had no idea that every step was taking him closer to an agonizing, horrifying death.

They would have to climb the steep staircase at the back of Ward No. 2 to reach the first floor. As he had planned, Navalkishore climbed steadily till he got to the top and then pretended to lose his footing and tumbled down the stairs.

The vat of boiling hot gruel promptly overturned, releasing a fiery stream of molten iron flowing out of a furnace. Lachman Singh didn't have the slightest chance to save himself. Set on fire by the boiling gruel and burnt to a crisp from head to toe, he rolled down the steps. By now the gruel had cooked his skin and flesh and was headed for his bones.

The pain was unbearable. Still Lachman Singh raced towards the pond in the middle of the jail, and jumped into the water. The news spread throughout the jail in a flash. Everyone went running up to the pond, pulling Lachman out of the water and carrying him to the hospital. The doctor layered antiseptic ointment on Lachman's body, now as white as an egg with his entire skin peeled off, and wrapped him in bandages. But Lachman did not survive. Groaning in pain all day, he died at eleven o' clock at night.

However, rejecting the claims of medical science, the guard on duty that night at the hospital declared firmly, 'Nahin, doctor sahib. Lachman did not die at eleven. He talked with me till three in the morning. He was in no pain at that time. He was fine. I was sitting at the gate, looking towards the pond. Suddenly someone came up behind me and put his hand on my shoulder, saying, e sipahi-ji, thoda khaini dena. When I turned around, I saw Lachman standing there, covered in bandages from head to toe.'

Lachman standing there! The doctor and several others who had seen the state he was in were astonished. What on earth was Ramvilas saying! How could Lachman possibly have been standing? He had been writhing in pain all day. They had

had to tie him down on the bed, lest he fall off. He was untied only the next day, after his death. How could he have stood up and walked to the gate at three in the morning? Ramvilas was prone to drinking. He hadn't imagined the whole thing, had he? Or maybe he was joking.

'Ram-ji ka kasam,' Ramvilas said, touching his throat, 'I'm telling the truth. What do I have to gain by lying? Lachman asked me for khaini. I said you're not well, go to bed. But he kept standing there, saying, where do I find that bastard Naval now? He killed me. I won't spare him.'

'He said all this?'

'You think I'm making it up?'

These things happened, apparently. Kanai Mandol, a guard on morning duty who lived near Bhangor police station, said, 'Nothing surprising about it. A man who dies at an inauspicious moment has a lot of powers after death. Just the other day, someone I knew had died. How do I tell you this... Just as we were putting a torch to the pyre, the dead body threw aside all the wood piled on him and sat up. Do you know how this was possible? Because of the timing of his death. Why should Lachman Singh not be able to get out of his bed then and walk around? It was Saturday, and on top of that a new moon night. Everyone knows that someone who dies at such an hour becomes a ghoul.'

So it was not the living version of Lachman but his spirit, intent on revenge, who had come up to Ramvilas.

No one came from Lachman Singh's village in Bihar to collect his corpse. His body rotted with a pile of others for some time, becoming bloated. No one knew what happened after that.

But the dead Lachman presented himself in jail as much more of a terrifying menace than when he was alive. He was often seen walking towards Ward No. 2 in the darkness, covered in bandages the way he was when he died. Sometimes he could be heard groaning piteously, 'Jal gaya!' At times he raced off from the ward towards the pond and plunged in.

It was a full moon night after an unbearably hot day. Rahman Mollah had been in charge at the chauka, being grilled by the heat from the enormous ovens. The door of his ward faced southward. A breeze filtered in through the bars of the thick iron gate. Not only was Rahman Mollah exhausted, but he had also smoked some ganja, which was why he was fast asleep.

Suddenly he felt someone tugging at his hair. Which bastard was it? As he shot up, his blood froze. Lachman Singh was standing outside, covered in milk white bandages. His eyes were blazing like balls of fire. One look and Rahman clamped his eyes shut before fainting in terror. In the brief moment he had been poised on the edge between consciousness and oblivion, he had heard Bandiswala roar, 'Where's my food?' Rahman remembered nothing after this. But the other prisoners woke up at his loud moaning. In utter consternation, they saw a figure in white walking around the ward. Moments later Rampada, the guard on duty, was heard saying in fear, 'Who's there?' There was no reply. Only the sound of something or someone plunging into the pond. Rampada came runing up to the gate of the ward. Discovering the lock still in place, he said, stupefied, 'The gate is locked! Who was it then?'

Everyone was awake by now. They were both frightened and astounded. All the prisoners were locked up at this hour. Only the guards were outside, stationed at their respective posts. No one but Rampada was supposed to be here. Since he was asking who it was, it obviously wasn't him. Who, then?

By then Rampada had come to. What he said after composing himself gave everyone a shock. But why had Bandiswala visited Rahman?

'Don't you get it?' Rampada said. 'Such idiots... Who is Rahman? He's in charge of the chauka. Which means he's in charge of all the food too, isn't he? So he came to Rahman to demand food. Who else would he ask? As far as he's concerned, he's still in jail. So he has his meals allotted to him. Yes or no? Is he wrong to ask for his due? It's not right to upset spirits. We'd better leave his food for him below the banyan tree from now on.'

This seemed reasonable to everyone. So the next night, a few parotas and some meat cooked with great care was left beneath the tree. The next morning, the plate was found cleaned out. Even the bones had been crunched.

What more proof did anyone need?

Rahman was no longer here. His sentence had ended. Rampada too had been transferred to some other jail. But the system of serving Bandiswala delicious meals every day had persisted. Whoever was put in charge of the kitchen had to ensure that the tradition was not broken.

FOUR

The sun has set some time ago. All the lights have been switched on, but a dim darkness pervades the jail. About fifteen prisoners are seated in a row in front of Deputy Jailer Mohinimohon-babu's desk. There are swellings on their bodies, twisted ankles, bruises beneath eyes. They were presented in the courts today, sent from police stations. Now they're in jail custody. The deputy jailer is checking their names and addresses against the court warrants and making entries in the register. They will be searched meticulously after the paperwork is done and then despatched to amdani, where they will spend the night.

Having entered the name of one of the under-trial prisoners, his father's name, and details of identification marks, the deputy jailer is preparing to inhale a pinch of snuff when something heavy strikes his feet. Groaning in pain, he looks at the floor to find a head, attached to a body, in the vicinity of his toes. In other words, someone is offering a pronaam to declare his devotion. Such extreme reverence is no longer in vogue. 'And who might you be?'

Getting back on his feet after demonstrating his veneration, the man grins and says, 'Eggey aami Bhogai. My name is Bhagoban, sir, Bhagoban Sardar.'

The deputy is startled at the appearance of Bhogai aka Bhagoban. A face as pointy as a mole's. Yellowed teeth that are not only competing for the same spot inside the mouth, but also straining to come out of it. Dressed in khaki trousers that undoubtedly belong to someone else. The baggy pants are tied at the waist with a length of cloth. A sleeveless banyan, with all the grime in the world settled on it. A thin, tall, thirtyish man of most peculiar appearance. 'And which Bhagoban might you be?'

'Don't you remember, sir? I was a faltu at amdani last time. You were very fond of me.'

At last the deputy jailer remembers. This was the faltu who had helped spot nearly half a kilo of ganja stashed away in amdani.

There's a clandestine business of liquor and ganja in the jail. Despite their best efforts, the authorities haven't succeeded in closing it down. Some of the guards are active in this enterprise. They bring packets of ganja into the jail and put them in the safekeeping of trusted prisoners. Whoever wants some can buy it from them. The currency varies. Prisoners in charge of the kitchen can pay with food. The prisoner who has the responsibility of entering records at the hospital – he's called the 'writer' – is also in charge of stocks of milk, butter, sugar, bread and biscuits. As for the prisoner in charge of the godown, he controls everything. The one in charge at amdani is responsible for distributing body-oil to prisoners. At eight grams per head, imagine the quantity of oil needed for three or four thousand inmates. Who's going to stop him from distributing only a part of his stocks and selling the rest? The point is, in a jail of this size, almost everyone gets a chance to make some extra money to pay for their nightly supply of intoxicants.

Even those who cannot make money on the side can find sources of pleasure. Paper and pen are available with the guards. Write a letter home. The guard will deliver it and collect the money you've requested for, keeping a hundred or two hundred for himself as compensation. What if they keep the entire amount? No, they won't be such traitors. They know you can betray the customer only once, but honesty brings repeat business.

Once, the prisoner in charge of amdani had tried to get into business on his own, bypassing the warder and guards. He had got hold of things to sell using his own resources, with a sweeper as his accomplice. The sweeper came in to clean the prison every day. He had concealed some cannabis in his broom and delivered it to amdani.

Somehow Bhagoban had got to know, and somehow Bhagoban had let the cat out of the bag for the benefit of the deputy jailer. No wonder Mohinimohon-babu's face is convulsed with happiness now at being reunited with the very same Bhagoban. 'Arre Bhagoban! You look absolutely different. I didn't recognise you at all.'

Bhagoban exudes bitterness. 'How will I stay the same, babu! Do you think I get to eat and sleep out there as regularly as in jail? One shoulder, a thousand responsibilities. My health is broken.'

'If it's such a difficult life being free,' laughed the deputy jailer, 'why bother to go out at all? Might as well stay in here. This is practically your own home.'

'You're right,' says Bhagoban humbly. 'But then, sir, it's not as simple as that. So much trouble getting in here. No chance of getting caught till I've sneaked into at least twenty-five homes to steal. You know what they say, people go to work every day, burglars only once in ten days. So just imagine, first there's no work for ten days at a stretch. Tachhara shobbai toh aar puleeshe daayna. Even if I get caught, some of them just beat me up instead of handing me over to the police. How do I get to jail then?'

'That's true.' A cunning smile appears beneath the deputy jailer's snuff-stained moustache. With an expression of deep sympathy, he says, 'But it's been a long while since you were here last. At least a year.'

'Oh no, can't be so long. You remember they came from the Manobseba Asrom last November and fed everyone sweets? I got out just after that. So about eight months.'

Bhagoban continues after a pause, 'When I got out of jail, I went home. I found my wife had run away, leaving my two-year-old son behind. My father died long ago. All I have is my mother. Old. Half blind. Barely survives selling cowdung. She could hardly manage a baby. How would she look after him if I went to jail again? Have you heard of Jhinki, babu? A big town near our village. With a missionary school. I tried very hard and got my son into the school. Nothing more to worry about. They'll take care of food, clothes, everything. All this took eight months.'

Paresh the 'writer' is seated next to the deputy jailer. His job is to maintain lists of who's due in court, who has meetings with visitors scheduled, and so on. The young handsome Paresh had eloped with the girl next door. He's now serving a sentence for abducting an underage woman.

'Tell me, Bhagoban,' he says, 'how many times have you been to jail?'

Bhagoban shakes his head. 'Can't say. Never counted. In and out since I was that high.' He holds his hand out, palm down, to indicate the height.

'Why do you like living a convict's life? Can't you steal something really valuable, something you can survive on for a year or two?'

Bhagoban fixes his eyes on Paresh. 'I'm poor. I don't know how the rich live. You're in jail. You eat here. You have no idea the state the villages are in. You think anyone has enough for me to steal? Scraps here, bones there, not even that. Don't have the heart to steal from them. If I take their rice, they'll starve. Things are not as they were. The villages are burning.'

'Can't accept that,' Paresh argues. 'How can everyone be poor? There must be some rich people. If not in one village, then in another, ten or twenty miles away.'

'There are,' says Bhagoban. 'Can't break in. All brick houses. No chance for thieves to get in. Only robbers. But what will they get? A couple of hundred in cash. Some brass stuff. No one's a fool. They put their money in banks. Banks everywhere. Why will they keep money at home. Theft or robbery, it doesn't pay anymore.'

After a pause Bhagoban continues, 'Once, I was this small, I went with my father to steal. Two years after the China war. Famine everywhere. Gormen thike ekhane okhane langorkhana khulise. All these government camps serving a spoonful of khichuri to everyone. Just like in jail. Two-mile-long queues. How to describe it, dada, millions dying of starvation. You've heard of Chowdhury-babu? They sacrifice a pair of oxen at Dugga Pujo. I went there to steal with my father...' Bhagoban stops to glance at the deputy jailer. 'You're government, sir. But still I can swear even your godowns don't have so much rice. So much! Mountains of rice. Sack upon sack upon sack upon sack. Thousands of sacks. They knew the famine was coming. So they bought rice from everywhere and hoarded it in their godowns. As prices rose, they...'

'Never mind all that, what did you do after getting in?'

'What do you suppose? My father put a half-filled sack on my head, picked up a full one himself. But bad luck. Couldn't go too far. Imagine walking seventeen or eighteen miles with sacks that way. The sun rose before we could reach home. The chowkidar caught my father.'

Bhagoban stops suddenly. 'And then?' Paresh pokes him.

'Tarpor aar ki, you know what happens when a thief is caught. My father took to his bed after that beating and never got up again. Died a month later.'

What began as a light story has taken a serious turn. Paresh is silent. The deputy jailer pipes up. 'Nobody's parents live forever. Don't be sad, Bhagoban. Your father may be gone, but we're here, aren't we? Stay with us. I'll take care of all your needs.'

Bhagoban bows his head in gratitude. He wants to offer another round of pronaam to the deputy jailer. This isn't a man, he's a god. He's ready to give Bhagoban a bed for the night. Three meals a day. On top of which, he's being so kind. Why can't the people outside be as wonderful?

'Wait a bit, Bhagoban,' the deputy jailer says. 'Let me finish with the others, then I have something to discuss with you. Nothing very difficult. Easy enough for you. Just wait here.'

He completes entering the records for all the prisoners. Then they go back out to the courtyard between the two gates to squat in rows. Two guards begin searching them. After about ten minutes of being frisked thoroughly, they are made to sit in another line. Doing this for fifteen people takes both time and patience.

When it's all done, the deputy jailer waves Bhagoban over to himself. 'Nothing too difficult,' he says in a low voice. 'I'm putting you in a cell.'

The cells are only for serious criminals and approvers. Why me then? Bhagoban's voice quavers. 'Why a cell, babu? Aami ki kono dosh korichi?'

'Don't be silly, why should you have committed a crime? This is for a different reason. You'll get everything you need, even a medical diet. Do you know what a medical diet is? Two half-eggs, half a litre of milk, half a pound of bread, ten grams of butter, thirty grams of sugar, ten grams of tea leaves.'

'I know, I know,' confirms Bhagoban. 'Even fruits sometimes.'

'Yes, you'll get all of these. And you don't have to do anything in return. Just keep your eyes and ears open, and inform me of what they say, the things they do. I'll send for you every other day. Can you do it?'

'But I don't know who I have to keep an eye on.'

'Oho, didn't I tell you? There are five Naxals in the cells. You know Naxals? Very bad people. They escape from jail whenever they can. You'll have to tell me about them.'

'All right.'

'All right? If they question you just say, I'm an approver, see, what if the other casewalas beat me up? So deputy-babu has put me in your cell. Don't forget. You mustn't give them any other explanation. You'll have to become one of them and find out all their secrets. Go get yourself frisked now. I'll explain everything to the jamadar.'

Bhagoban is body-searched like all others. He is the last one. Once the guards are reassured none of them has a knife or razor or bomb or gun or narcotics or anything illegal on them, there is another headcount before they are herded into the jail. They will now go to amdani. There will be another round of frisking there, which is much worse than the one at the gate. They will be draped in towels, the foreskin of their penises will be peeled back, their testicles will be pressed, finger will probe deep into their anuses – all this to check for money, gold or gems hidden away somewhere. Anything that's found in the process is part of the earnings of the prisoner in charge of amdani.

There's no food tonight for these new arrivals. If anyone who went from the jail to court was released, that person's meal might be given to one of the newcomers.

Arriving at amdani, the jamadar selects one of the keys from the bunch hanging at this waist and unlocks the gate. Normally the keys are distributed among different people during the day, depending on requirements, but after the evening headcount, the keys to all the wards, cells, the hospital and everywhere else are deposited at the main gate. The jamadar collects them as needed.

Unlocking the gate of the amdani ward, the jamadar says, 'Saab ghoos ja. All of you except Bhagoban. You have to go to the cells.' The jamadar shepherds the prisoners in one by one, locks the gate behind them, and says, 'Come on, Bhagoban.'

Bhojon Biswas is on duty at the entrance to the cells. Neither the other guards nor the prisoners take the tall, dark and imbecilic looking Bhojon seriously. Nor does he particularly want to be an important player in the drama of the jail. He turns up on time, keeps himself to himself, does his work, and leaves. Normally there are always a few guards looking for a chance to beat up prisoners on the smallest of pretexts. But Bhojon is their antithesis. He doesn't even scold anyone for minor errors. This very Bhagoban had once overturned a bucket of oil he was ferrying from amdani to one of the wards. Any of the other guards would have skinned him alive. But Bhojon, who was on duty, only said, 'Tchah, you've gone and spilled it all.'

The jamadar walks past Bhojon to unlock the gate to the

cells. Bhagoban follows him. He sees five faces behind five small iron gates. The cells have no arrangement for electric lights. No one knows why. A lantern glows dimly outside each of them, far enough to be out of reach of the prisoners inside. Bhagoban knows the lanterns barely contain any oil. Even if you could get hold of one, there wouldn't be enough oil to set yourself on fire. These lanterns are lit in amdani and then brought here. All this used to be Bhagoban's responsibility once. The cells had other inmates then.

The five young men are standing at their cell doors, singing. It's a song of hope, love, trust and freedom for the world. All of them have their eyes closed. Their spines are erect, their voices resonant. Their environment has had no effect on them. Taut and fearless, they are singing the Internationale, the theme song of the communists.

> Arise, ye workers from your slumber,
> Arise, ye prisoners of want.
> For reason in revolt now thunders,
> and at last ends the age of cant!
>
> Away with all your superstitions,
> Servile masses, arise, arise!
> We'll change henceforth the old tradition,
> And spurn the dust to win the prize!
>
> So comrades, come rally,
> And the last fight let us face.

The Internationale
Unites the human race.

While they do their work, the jamadar does his. Unlocking the empty cell in the corner, he pushes Bhagoban in and locks the door behind him.

There is no window to let fresh air or light into these five-by-seven cells, so that no one can use a garment or a piece of cloth to fashion a noose from the bars and elude the Indian judicial system. A few months of this solitary tormented existence is fully capable of convincing a prisoner that death is a better option. There's reason to be cautious.

There is no furniture in the cells – only a pan for urine and stool, two blankets, a pitcher of water, a plate and a bowl. This cell has not been occupied in a long time. Because it has not been swept, there is a thick layer of dust on the floor. Bhagoban is lying on his back on a blanket. After several days of unbearable physical agony and mental tension, this night has arrived with its freedom from anxiety. No more worries. The routine of food, rest, conviviality, music, endless leisure and happiness will be resumed tomorrow.

The young men are still singing. When they're done, Bhagoban hears someone from the adjacent cell trying to draw his attention. 'O notun dada, shunte pachho? Can you hear me?' After the question has been asked several times, Bhagoban responds, 'I can. Tell me.'

'What's the case against you?'

No prisoner likes revealing directly what he's in for. He

mentions the section or sub-section of the Indian Penal Code under which he's been put in jail. So Bhagoban says, '380.'

'What did you steal?'

'A couple of cows.'

The most respected section of the IPC in the jail is 302, or murder. This is followed by 395, or robbery. 380, amounting to petty theft, is a matter of contempt, especially when it comes to stealing cows. The most hated are 376 and 420. One is for rape, and the other, for cheating. But thanks to Naxals, 302 has lost some of its exalted position. Whether it's the prisoners or the guards, the official enemy or the secret ally, it is the Naxals who are the centre of attention now.

The young man in the cell next to Bhagoban's is Bijon. 'If it's 380, why are you in here?' he asks. 'Aren't those cases supposed to go to the wards?'

Worried about giving the game away, Bhagoban answers, 'I don't know why. No one can read their minds. Now that I'm in jail, what choice do I have? I have to stay where they say, eat what they say, whether it's burnt food or the medical diet. Can't refuse.'

'All right. Get some rest now. We'll talk again in the morning.' After a pause Bijon says, 'You can't have got any food today. I have some ruti-torkari. Want some?'

'What will you eat if you give me your food?' Bhagoban says.

'They give four rutis. I won't starve if I have two instead of all four.' Bijon makes a packet of food with a sheet of writing paper and tosses it out of his cell through the door to where

Bhagoban can reach out and collect it. It's impossible for a starving man not to accept food. He finishes the food, drinks his fill of water, and lies down again on his back.

This is when Bhagoban is reminded of his wife and son. The boy at least will be fine in a missionary school. Maybe he won't recognise his father when he grows up. Let him not, but let him live. He would have died of starvation had he stayed with his grandmother. But what about his wife? Where had she disappeared without telling anyone? What unknown place had hunger taken her to? There was no greater enemy than an empty stomach. Hunger could rob a person of all love and affection and sympathy and make them inhuman. Could a mother abandon her baby otherwise?

Shantibala had pleaded with him through her tears many times. 'Don't go in for this stealing business anymore. Both of us can work. I want to eat without guilt. Everytime you go to jail, all these men proposition me. I can still take hunger, I can't take this. If you don't stop all this stealing, you'll see one day I've either hanged myself or gone away.'

She had been as good as her word. She had left. Never mind. That didn't trouble Bhagoban as much as the fact that she had blamed him needlessly. She had been too upset to realise he had not chosen to steal things out of choice. Why would he have chosen to be a petty thief if he could have found some work, something to get them two meals a day? No one would. Who enjoys being beaten up every time you're caught? Still you had to bear it. Because Bhagoban had not been able to fight his hunger. When he was starving, he could steal anything that came to hand. He was not concerned whether he would live or die if caught.

He had tried to make an honest living. But who was going to employ the son of a thief? In case anyone did, and then something went missing, whether it be a plate or glass or a hen or duck, everyone would assume it was Bhagoban. He would be punished despite his innocence.

Purkait of Hatkhola was one of those clever ones to take advantage of this. During the crop season, he had made Bhagoban work like a dog, giving him a few scraps to eat to keep him alive. Then, when it was time to pay his wages, Purkait claimed his wife's necklace was missing. 'It must be you, Bhagoban. Give it back or I won't pay you a rupee.'

Bhagoban had lost all interest in honest work since then. Not even Shanti's tears had motivated him.

He sinks into sleep eventually, these thoughts still swirling in his head, waking up several hours later to the sound of the guards shouting, 'File! File!' Time for the first headcount. The inmates of the wards will line up in pairs. But Bhagoban and the other five occupants of the cells will not have to step out. They cannot lie inanimate, but all they have to do is to move to indicate to the jamadar that they are alive. Bhagoban knows the drill. He stretches, and the jamadar leaves after the headcount.

About half an hour later, the siren rings. The gates to the cells are opened. One by one, the occupants come out. Porimal, Goutam, Bijon, Nemai, Bablu and Bhagoban. The faltu assigned to the cells has arrived by now. He takes the case tickets of the five Naxal prisoners to the hospital to fetch their medical diet.

None of the five was in favour of accepting any of the special benefits. But they had to give in to the insistence of Pagla Daktar. He had visited them in their cells the very next day after their arrival. Porimal and the rest of them had been in jail before. 'The doctor at the last jail had never bothered to examine us even if we went to the hospital. And you're actually visiting us in our cells? We're really surprised.'

'Surprised? Why? Why are you surprised? Aren't you the ones who talk of Dr Norman Bethune or Dr Kotnis? Aren't you the ones? What do they say? The patients mustn't visit the doctor, it's the doctor who must visit the patients. I've read in the papers how they brought you here. You can't possibly be well after that. Can't possibly be well. So I came to see you. It's my duty. Now I want to hear your problems one by one. Problems. One by one.'

'We don't have any particular problems. Just a few niggles.'

'You, what's your name? Do you get dizzy? Dizzy, is that what you feel sometimes? Do you feel weak? You have to. Given your height, your weight should be between fifty-eight and sixty-two. It's not, I know. I know it's not. Get your history ticket. Get it.'

The doctor didn't stop at prescribing a medical diet for Bijon. Within a month, he had shifted all five of them to the same diet. His practised eyes had diagnosed all of them as feeble and unwell. When Porimal objected, he said angrily, 'No one's father pays for it. This diet hasn't been paid for by anyone's father. Millions of people in the county pay taxes. Taxes are collected. What does your father do? A teacher? He pays taxes too. So do I, professional tax. That's where the money spent on all these policemen and the military and jails comes from. Your father's money is part of it. That's what's paying for your diet. No one else's father is paying for it.'

The faltu for the cells collects the tea leaves, milk and sugar assigned to the five of them and takes them to the kitchen. He returns to the cells with cups of tea. They ask Bhagoban to join them. 'Come, notun dada, have some tea with us. There's nothing else to do here.'

Bhagoban is hesitant. Something pricks at his conscience. 'Never mind,' he says.

'Why? Don't you drink tea?'

'Can't say I don't. I do when I can.'

'Then why not now?'

'No, it's just that...' Bhagoban says timidly, 'you already gave me your food last night. I was too hungry to say no. Now how can I have your tea again?'

Bablu laughs. 'This isn't food, this is just a drink. Those who drink together think together.'

'You're right,' Bhagoban responds. 'They say you have to taste just one grain in the pot to understand how good the rice is. Last night I got to know all of you because of what one of you did for me. As it is people don't get enough to eat in jail. Still you starved yourself to let me eat. No one will share even a bidi here, and you gave me half your food. Nobody does it.'

'The tea's getting cold,' Bijon reminds him. 'We can talk about all this while we have it.'

Bhagoban accepts the glass of tea they offer him, but he doesn't take a sip. 'All right, I'll have the tea because you're giving it to me. But will you keep my request? It's in your interest.'

'What request?'

'Keep all your conversations secret. Make sure I don't overhear anything.'

'Why not?'

Stammering, Bhagoban says, 'Na, maane tomra toh amare thik chenona aami kerom. You have no idea what I'm like. What if I'm the one whom deputy babu told: Bhagoban, we've known you for such a long time, we like you very much. There's something you must do for us. We know it's hard, but stay in the cells for a few days. We'll give you everything you need. All you have to do is listen to their conversations and pass everything on to us. Now since I'm taking a favour from him, I must follow his instructions, mustn't I?'

'You must.'

'So if you reveal any secrets to me, I have to divulge them to him. You'll be in trouble then. You're good people. You're serving jail sentences to help others. You're not doing it for yourselves, you're doing it for the nation. If you come to harm because of me, I won't find peace even in death.'

'All right, all right, drink up your tea now,' Bijon reminds Bhagoban.

FIVE

Here in Bengal the cat is referred to as the tiger's aunt. Whether it applies to other cats or not, the name is eminently applicable to Haloom the cat. He is as fat as he is tall. He has been living in the jail for about three years.

The jail is infested with rats. Small, medium, large – thanks to rats of all sizes, the sacks of rice, wheat and dal stored in the godown are never safe. The rats gnaw away at the jute with their tiny teeth. Who knows what pleasure this game affords them. Meanwhile their droppings, grime and dust mix freely with the grains and pulses to make everything inedible.

It was to safeguard against this invasion of rodents that Shurjo-babu the godown clerk had picked Haloom up from the streets and taken him in. The glassy-eyed cottonball-white Haloom had found himself an enormous hunting ground as a result. Where the prey numbered in thousands and there was just one hunter.

He was conscious of his responsibilities initially, killing four or five rats every day. But this unlimited supply of meat was his downfall. He became corpulent, and as his age rose, so did his laziness. He can no longer chase his prey with the alacrity of the past. He cannot pounce on them with sharp claws. And so he has lost the wish to do it too. He knows he is the only emperor of his gigantic kingdom. Hundreds of humans live here. He can secure his own sustenance with very little effort at the chauka and amdani where food for the humans is available. Then why bother with hunting? With no wife or children or household to maintain, why work so hard when the only person he had to feed was himself?

Tonight Haloom is sleeping amidst the iron bars in the condemned godown. He wakes up at around one in the morning with pangs of hunger. But where will he get any food now? The kitchen was emptied out in the evening. The labourers washed the dishes after distributing the food and left. The only place where he might find some food is amdani. If fifty people went to the courts today and fifteen or twenty of them came back, amdani should be full of food. No harm checking.

Haloom saunters off in that direction. The guard on duty at the wall next to the condemned godown is asleep. The poor man can hardly be blamed. The flock of nine of ten buffaloes in front of the barracks belongs to him. He has a hard time all day, bathing them, milking them, distributing the milk to shops. He has no time to sleep during the day. He's combining his duty hours with sleeping hours now.

Haloom strolls in silence along the path between two wards to arrive at the case-table. The stores godown is next to amdani, near the gate. Three huge locks hang on its door. All the thieves and robbers are locked in the wards. Those who roam around free are not thieves but guards. Who has the godown been secured from?

Haloom isn't bothered about any of this. He goes directly to amdani, and looks around with eyes glowing like marbles. A 60-watt bulb is hanging inside. Its light has created a ghostly atmosphere in the corners of the room. He can also see there isn't an inch of space inside, amdani is chock-a-bloc with people. Good heavens! So many people being sent to jail these days! Why? Don't they have any other place to go?

Never mind all that. The question is, how to get in? At least eight people are sprawled directly in front of the door. But still, there's a way. There's some space beneath the only window. If he can jump on the sill, slip through the bars and leap, he can vault over Jalodhar, who is in charge at amdani tonight, and land near the pitcher of water. If there's any food, that's where it will be. Even if nothing particularly delicious is available, there should at least be some fish bones. There was fish for dinner today.

No matter how often a prisoner has been to jail, he can never sleep the first few nights. The ghastly memories of the road to the jail pursue him all the time. He cannot rest for anxiety about the future. All that he can achieve in this state can at best be called dozing. A larger number of people are dozing on the floor of amdani right now.

Haloom jumps gently on to the window sill and pokes his head in through the bars. Calculating the distance, he makes his leap. But his calculations have gone awry. Instead of covering the distance he meant to, he lands squarely on Jalodhar's chest. The sudden impact of a heavy object breaks Jalodhar's light sleep. 'Aaaaaaah!' he screams. Everyone wakes up at his anguished cry. Those of them who have been to this jail before and know of Bandiswala open their sleep-laced eyes to find...Bandiswala! He may have shrunk his body, but he has made no attempt to hide his white bandages and his blazing eyes. He is attacking Jalodhar with all his fury. In panic they add their screams to Jalodhar's. Aaaaaaah! Hearing them, the remaining prisoners start screaming in unison without having the slightest idea of what's going on. Aaaaaaah!

Haloom was not expecting this. He is disconcerted by this thunderstorm of wails. Cancelling his plans, he leaps back towards the window and disappears through the bars.

But disaster has struck by then. It's as though a match has been held to a dry haystack. The fire is spreading from one stack to the next.

The frightened screams from amdani have reached Wards 3 and 4. In jail parlance, these two are the chhokra files. Younger prisoners are kept there. All of them begin to scream for their lives. The panic spreads across the jail. Everyone thinks they will be attacked and throttled to death any moment. All of them begin wailing in mortal fear of their impending demise – save me, save me, save me! The guards on duty are flabbergasted and start shouting and running about in disarray.

It wasn't Haloom's fault. Everyone here is always on tenterhooks. He was merely the stray spark that started the conflagration. For several minutes, the heartrending cries of terrified prisoners are heard across the length and breadth of the jail.

Finally a single voice of courage is heard amidst all this. It belongs to Bhojon Biswas, the guard on duty at the cells. 'Ei! What's the matter? What are all of you screaming for?'

'Bandiswala!' someone sobs in a stricken tone from the first floor of Ward No. 1.

'Kothaye re? Where's this Bandiswala?' Bhojon bangs on the floor with his stick and abandons his position in front of the cells to come forward. Meanwhile, two or three other guards on night duty have come running up to the pool of light near the case-table. The newcomers are still crying in amdani, but the screaming has quietened to sobbing. The faltu at amdani is sprinkling water on Jalodhar's face. When he comes to, he says, 'It's nobody's fault but mine. My bad luck.' Then he explains that last year he had a test identification parade, where the accused person is made to stand in a line with nine others. If the witnesses cannot identify him in this line-up of ten people, the case against him is weakened. Usually identification becomes difficult when there are so many people to choose from.

Jalodhar has been accused of stealing a taxi. If he had been successful, he could have carried out the robbery he was planning with the help of the vehicle, but luck was against him. Chased by a crowd while trying to escape, he drove into a pothole and was caught.

The taxi-driver was supposed to turn up for the identification. There was no doubt that he would identify

Jalodhar. Because the officer in charge at the police station had personally brought them face-to-face, telling the taxi-driver, 'Look at him carefully. You'll have to identify him in a line-up of ten people three months from now. He'll look different then. His hair and beard will have grown. If you cannot identify him, the case will collapse.'

Having no other resort, Jalodhar had sought intervention not from the judge or from the lawyer, but from Bandiswala. 'My lord Bandiswala, there's nowhere you cannot go, nothing you cannot do. Save me, o Lord. I will give you a pair of coconuts if the taxi-driver fails to identify me.' The prayer had worked. The taxi-driver couldn't spot Jalodhar in the line-up despite the close scrutiny earlier.

Now it was time to fulfill the terms of the vow. But Jalodhar had not been able to get hold of coconuts in jail despite his best efforts. Systematically saving a little of the body-oil handed out every day to the prisoners, he had managed to provide five kilograms of oil to a guard. But the guard conveniently forgot his promise to get Jalodhar his coconuts. Eventually Jalodhar forgot too. The debtor can always forget. He has nothing to lose. But the creditor remembers. And today he was here to settle accounts.

'I was on cell duty, you fool,' says Bhojon Biswas. 'I could see the window of amdani from my post. It was no ghost, it was Haloom. He leapt off and ran away when all of you began screaming.'

The amdani ward, in fact not just the amdani ward but the entire jail, is split down the middle over this. One group has accepted Bhojon Biswas's argument. The other says there's nothing that spirits cannot do. They can take on the appearance of cats if they want to, or of buffaloes, or even of nothing at all. They can turn into the wind and do as they please.

SIX

Morning. The inmates are strolling around the yard in front of their wards after the doors have been unlocked. Of the fourteen wards in this building, the most significant one is No. 10. Around fifteen political prisoners are held captive here. All of them are well educated. In the outside world, some of them are teachers, some journalists, some doctors and engineers. They have been arrested from different places on charges of sedition. The authorities hold them in high regard. They never dare treat them the way they treat ordinary prisoners.

Political prisoners are also housed in Ward No. 7. Other prisoners are forbidden from speaking to them. The authorities fear that iron which sticks too long to magnets becomes magnetic itself. The fear isn't entirely unfounded. Investigations of the incidents that these prisoners have sparked off in this jail have revealed that in each case, a class of ordinary prisoners and even a section of employees have been involved. Hence the additional caution.

Almost everyone in No. 7 is a young man. Some of them are students, and others, educated and unemployed. Yet others dropped out of college on the principle that the more one is educated in a bourgeois system, the more ignorant one becomes. Instead, they plunged into the revolutionary act of capturing the state machinery by surrounding the city with villages. There are also workers from small factories, as well as discontented sons of farmers. They are an endless headache for the jail authorities. Disobedient, fearless, belligerent and reckless, they are capable of any act. Both killing and dying are child's play to them.

When it comes to these prisoners, the jailer and his team are perpetually on their guard. And these inmates are under watch round the clock. The surveillance is conducted both by sleuths paid for the job as well as unpaid pairs of eyes. One of which belongs to Bashudeb, who's in charge of the godown. Not everyone knows he's a spy, only the jailer and his deputy do. He has been instructed to mix with the group till he can't be told apart from them. This involves agreeing with them about everything. 'They have to consider you one of them. That's when you'll get all the real news.' Bashu had complied. He had become one of them.

Bhagoban knows nothing about Bashu. So when he parts with what he thinks is vital information – 'I don't like this Bashu's ways, babu. He's no longer a chor-chhyanchor, he's become a 100 per cent noskal' – the deputy jailer pays no attention. 'All right, we'll worry about him later. Give me other news.'

Bhagoban has been in jail for just a month. Already 'officers' from Lalbazar have interrogated him four times. Apparently he has turned approver in a case. Every time he's interrogated, he goes back to the cell with cigarettes, soap, body-oil. Today is one of those days.

'What are you doing, Bhagoban, you haven't given us anything useful even after a month,' says the deputy jailer. 'Give us some real news.'

'What can I tell you,' Bhagoban says glumly. 'They're very clever. They don't say a thing when I'm there. If someone has to say something in secret to someone else, they scribble a note and pass it to the person, who reads it quickly. I'm illiterate, how will I know what...'

'They communicate through written notes?'

'Written. Sometimes in inlis too. How am I supposed to cope with such tricks?'

The deputy jailer takes a pinch of snuff. This is essential when tackling complex problems. Snuff enables him to think clearly.

'All right, you can't understand what they say or write, but at least you can observe what they do. Haven't you noticed anything to suggest they're conspiring?'

'I have,' answers Bhagoban at once. 'Everything they do seems like a conspiracy to me.'

'Do they talk to the other prisoners?'

'Everyone has to take the same road to the toilet. One or two at that time... Bashu's the one who talks the most, smiles the most. Why all this peeriti with noskal people? Why is he so fond of them?'

'And the guards? Do they chat with the guards?'

'Not much. The guards are afraid of them. You know, that one, Porimal. Seems he knifed a policeman and grabbed his gun. What if he does it again? Puleesh, shepai, both are scared of him. But there's one, Bhojon the guard. He isn't afraid, he chats with them.'

'Do they pass letters through the guards?'

'Never seen that.'

'All right. Keep watching closely, all right?' Before handing Bhagoban over to a guard to be escorted back to his cell, the deputy jailer says, 'Is everything OK? Are you getting the medical diet properly?'

'I am,' nods Bhagoban. 'Getting everything, no problem. Just one problem: staying alone in a cell is so hard, I wonder how they do it year after year.'

'Stay another month. See if you can get some secret information. I'll send you to a ward after that.'

Bhagoban runs into Bashu on his way back to his cell. Bashu first came to the jail the last time Bhagoban was inside. Three RPF case. Meaning he stole something from a train. Basu doesn't look like he's capable of unscrewing fans or cutting cables or gathering aluminium sheets. Some people say he was leaving with paper and plastic scraps, torn slippers and other discarded things, when he found a bearing from a goods train in a bush, hidden there by some other thief, and was caught when he tried to sell it.

Any prisoner under trial is usually made to slave on his first day in jail. Take water to all the wards. Clean the place.

Bhagoban had made Bashu, the new arrival, work very hard, getting him to clear out all the garbage from amdani. Something like ragging freshers in college.

Then Bashu was transferred to Ward No. 3. There was someone named Mityun there, whom he had known outside, who was posted in the godown. Mityun pulled some strings to get Bashu to work in the godown too. When Mityun was sent to another jail after three months, Bashu became the boss of the godown. The warehouse clerk, Shurjo-babu, trusted him implicitly, claiming that Bashu was a thief outside but as honest as Judhishthir inside. Bashu goes to the jail gate every morning, waiting for Shurjo-babu to arrive with the keys so that he can unlock the godown. Measuring out the supplies needed in the kitchen that day, he returns to the main gate. There he receives the deliveries. All this takes him till eleven in the morning, after which he returns to his ward for a bath, lunch, and a nap. He reopens the warehouse in the afternoon, sends the supplies needed for the night's meal to the kitchen, and then drops by at the gate again for a chat over cups of tea. But one day a week, Friday, when the guards collect their rations, he has to work late into the night. The guards get their rations at the gate. Rice, wheat, sugar. Bashu conscripts some other prisoners to help carry the sacks to the gate, where he measures out everyone's rations for them.

Shurjo-babu may not be aware, but Bhagoban knows that Bashu makes a little something from every single activity. When he measures out the portions for the kitchen, he sends ten kilos of oil instead of the eight needed. The extra two kilos are split between him and whoever is in charge of the chauka. Every item of food is smuggled away this way. Bashu gets bribes from the suppliers at the gate who provide less material, and inferior at that, than they're paid for. The guards also slip him a little money so that they can take away more rations than they're entitled to. Other than the person in charge of the kitchen, no one in this jail earns as much as Bashu.

Bhagoban thinks it's because of his earnings that Bashu refuses to get out of jail. Three RPF is hardly a serious charge. He can send any of the guards to the court with two hundred rupees for a lawyer to get him bail. But he doesn't.

Now Bashu sees Bhagoban and chuckles. 'How are you, you cow thief?'

This is the time for the prisoners' 'interviews' – when they meet their relatives and friends. There's a room split by a wire mesh on one side of the office. The prisoners stand one one side of the mesh, their visitors on the other. Each of them gets ten minutes. Ten prisoners at a time this side, twenty or thirty of their visitors on the other. A gap of six or seven feet between them. Everyone wants to discuss important things, so there is an enormous din as a result of all the people speaking loudly and even shouting in order to be heard. Not everything that is said is actually heard. The allotted ten minutes pass by in a sweaty flood of weeping, accusations and curses.

Bashu never appears at these meetings. His family comes by in the morning if they need to talk to him. It's possible to have a quiet conversation at the gate. Bhagoban knows that this is when Bashu hands over all that he has earned. The transaction is simple. Banwari, who brings the cart laden with vegetables to the jail, takes the money from Bashu and passes it to his relatives.

These days Bashu has begun to throw his weight around. See how much power I have, he seems to be telling his fellow inmates. I go where I like and smoke cigarettes. Bhagoban could have done it too. But he doesn't, to honour Deputy-babu's request. Just a few days more. Then he'll see.

Getting no response from Bhagoban, Bashu taunts him, 'I heard you're going to be egrari, you cow thief.'

Rapists and cattle thieves have no respect in jail. But an even more heinous crime is to be egrari – to confess your crime to the judge in court. An accused person who does this is a coward, a traitor. It doesn't matter what you say to the police to avoid being beaten up, but if you confess like Charandas Chor in court, what awaits you in jail is hatred, abuse and contempt. Bhagoban wasn't angry on being called a cow-thief, but being accused of being egrari makes him furious. It's natural to be enraged when false allegations are made. Deputy-babu can use the English term 'approver', but actually it is the equivalent of losing your caste.

'Your father's egrari,' Bhagoban snarls back. 'Your mother's egrari. Your whole bloody family is egrari. What should I be egrari for. I've been in jail from the time you had snot running down your nose. No khankir chhabal, no son of a whore can ever claim I confessed in court.'

The guard tries to intervene. 'Let's go, let's go. Old friend. Bola toh kya hai. Just joking. Don't fight.'

'What if he said it?' Bhagoban rages in his head. 'Didn't tell you, did he? Why should it bother you? Have you any idea? It's a slur, a terrible insult. A prisoner can't be accused of doing anything worse than confessing in court. The lawyer who takes a bribe from the opposite side to lose his case deliberately, the solider who takes a bullet in his back while fleeing – they are traitors to their professions, and so is a professional criminal who becomes egrari.'

As he returns to his cell with the guard, Bhagoban reflects that what he has done was not wise. Who knows whether it's spread all over the jail by now. Will he be able to hold his head high anymore? He has no standing as a human being outside jail. Thief, son of a thief, is how everyone describes him. Chorer chhele chor. Whatever respect he commanded was in jail, but now that's gone too. All his own fault. What will Bhagoban live on now?

Those who have never been to jail, who are not criminals by nature, do not know that no matter how many stories and plays and films are created about the truthful Charandas Chor in the world outside, declaring him a great man, in the universe of crime he is nothing but a gandu, an arsehole.

Bhagoban has heard stories about Charandas from his cellmates. He used to steal, but he also used to tell the truth, and keep his word even if it meant risking his life. This was what led him into danger, eventually killing him. He escaped by dying, for had he gone to jail instead, he would have had to live with even greater ignominy.

Bhagoban is not a real approver, he is a fake one. But now

he cannot say this to anyone. He feels miserable. Back in his cell, he flops down in a corner without a word to anyone and buries his face in his knees. The other prisoners are walking up and down in the corridor outside. There's still an hour and a half to go to lock-up. They exercise as much as they can to keep their bodies and minds active. Seeing him slumped in a corner, Nemai says, 'What is it, Bhagoban-dada, why so upset?'

Bhagoban almost starts sobbing. 'I've lost all my honour. Everything is gone. Shobbonash hoye geiche.'

'What's the matter, tell me.'

'What good is it telling you. It's my own fault. How can I tell anyone of the shit I've swallowed because I didn't know what I was doing? No wonder Bhushan and Hablo and Tarapado stare at me that way. No one talks to me, they only stare. What does it mean? They're all condemning me.'

'You haven't done anything to be condemned for.'

'I have, I have. You have no idea.'

Bijon tries to change the subject. 'Who came to interrogate you today, Bhagoban-da? What did he ask?'

'What can he ask?' Bhagoban lifts his eyes like an angry cat. 'The same questions. I hate having to say the same thing every day.'

Bijon realises Bhagoban does not want to go into the details. Pressuring someone to reveal something they would rather not creates more problems than it solves. 'Are they the ones who gave you the soap and oil?' he asks instead.

'They have to. You know what they say. A cat climbs a tree when there's trouble on the ground.'

Suddenly they hear someone walking along the road outside the cell towards the toilet, banging on a plate with a spoon as he sings a song. There are no mugs in the toilets. Prisoners have to pour water into the plates they eat out of and take them in. The water has to be collected from the pond. The plate is empty now, which is why the singer can beat on it with his spoon. The song is his own composition:

> Ore mon monre amaar
> Goruchor egrari holo
> Sheijonno taar poran gelo
> Ore mon monre amaar
>
> Oh my heart, oh my heart
> When cow thief turns approver
> His poor soul is split apart
> Oh my heart, oh my heart

The guard on duty at the cell bursts out laughing. 'Saala always happy in jail, always singing.' Bhagoban recognises the singer's voice. It's Gosain, not Bashu. The bastard went singing devotional songs from house to house and stole things whenever he could. He was making off with a police officer's watch when caught. Had a serious case slapped on him. Not released even after two years. 'If you get bail, I'll arrest you at the jail gate for murder,' the officer has told him.

The police can do such things nowadays. They have a lot of power. Rambabu was in jail for four years without trial. Twenty-three cases. Every time he got bail for one case, the police slapped two more on him. Eventually his lawyer appealed to the court to hear all the cases against his client together. About to leave after getting bail in all his cases, old and new, Rambabu found the police waiting at the gate with ropes. Picking him up, they hid him somewhere for a few days, meanwhile bringing two new cases against him and taking him back to the jail. Bhagoban remembers what the tall officer with the red face had said during the re-arrest. 'No one can save you, Rambabu. You will rot in jail. I'm the only one who can save you, but for that you have no choice but to accept my conditions.' Rambabu had not agreed. But he hadn't returned to this jail either, he had been taken elsewhere. The newspapers had written about the whole thing.

Another incident took place at that time. The police advised a certain lawyer not to represent a particular person accused in a particular case. This will work to your advantage, they told him. The lawyer was fond of his drink. He responded spiritedly, 'I'm in the business of law. It is my business to entertain the legal needs of anyone who comes to me.' So the police waited for their opportunity. One night they nabbed him on his way out of a bar. He was handcuffed and hauled into court in the presence of hundreds of people. The accusation was a dangerous one. He was supposed to have assaulted a police sergeant in a drunken state. A bottle and a ripped khaki uniform were produced as evidence...

Now Gosain's singing infuriates Bhagoban. 'Rotting for two years?' he says in his head. 'Rot for two more. May your case files be lost. Die!'

Shahodeb Mandol had been accused of stealing twenty-five kilos of salt. His case file was lost in the courts. He didn't get a hearing for eleven months. The trial didn't even begin. No one came to see him. He got no soap or oil. Scabs and sores appeared on his body. Thousands of lice, known in jail parlance as chillar, were found in his clothes. Eventually Shahodeb went on hunger strike on the advice of the Naxals. Finally the jail authorities took the initiative to inform the court. And Shahodeb was released…

Bhagoban lies down on the floor of his cell. He hates everything now. The pain is eating away at him. 'It's a big mistake I've made, a big mistake,' he mutters.

Porimal pauses outside his cell. 'All human beings make mistakes. Only the devil does not. A true human being learns from his mistake and chooses the correct path.'

'What lesson should I learn, tell me,' says Bhagoban despondently. 'What is this correct path? My entire life is threaded with mistakes. I'm wracked with pain. You know the saying, koyla jay na dhuli, shobhab jay na moli. Coal can't be cleaned, habits can't be killed.'

'Not true,' says Porimal. 'Coal can in fact be cleaned, and habits can be killed too. When a habit is the result of poverty and scarcity, you just have to get rid of those two things to kill the habit. And as for coal, why would you wash it? Throw it into a fire, all the black will burn away, leaving behind what's pure and white. You must also learn to burn the black out of your life. Done properly, you might dazzle everyone with the light.'

Porimal continues after a pause, 'Thousands of people like you and me are living on earth at this moment. Some of them will live fifty years, some a hundred. But then they will die. No one will remember them a month later. But a man who dies selflessly for his country, for millions of other people, will not be forgotten even after hundreds of years. Which is greater? To live a century like sheep, or to die with your head held high like a man? Which is preferable?'

Goutam comes up next to Porimol. 'Make it simple,' he signals.

'Sorry,' Porimal corrects himself. 'Which one is better, Bhagoban-dada? Take Goutam here, his father is a manager in a tea garden. He can get bail right now with a single signature on an affidavit. But why is he suffering here in jail? Because he has seen the extreme poverty of the workers on the tea estate with his own eyes. And he has also seen the opulent lifestyles and heartlessness of the rich men who suck everything out of the workers. This has turned him into a revolutionary. I'm often astonished, it hurts me, sometimes I'm in despair, when I see that these middle-class young men are fighting so hard, even dying, but the people for whom they are doing all this are not doing anything for themselves. They're not even asking, what are these young men saying? Why are they saying these things?'

Bhojon Biswas is standing at the door to the cells. Shaking his head, he says, 'But I've heard you say them. How is it that none of you is afraid of me?'

'Why should we be afraid?' Porimal laughs. 'We're not hatching a secret plot. Really, Bhojon-da, people surprise me.

They're dying like animals without food and drink, but they don't want to know why they're dying.'

Porimal goes back to addressing Bhagoban. 'Tell me, Bhagoban-dada, does it never occur to you? So many people don't get even a mouthful to eat, while so many others, who have never shed a drop of sweat in their lives, own millions. They spend thousands of rupees every day without a second thought.'

'I'm an ignorant man. How will I know these things? How will I understand them?'

'Have you even tried to know? It is because we don't know, because we don't understand, that we are in this sorry state today. We don't have to think of others. If we even thought of ourselves, if we loved only ourselves, we wouldn't have been so blind. It is for our own needs that the social trash must be eradicated. Unless a society that's rotted and become poisonous can be cleansed, how is it possible to have healthy, beautiful lives?'

Bhagoban does not respond. He does not have the words. These are educated people. They've read so many books. They're bound to know everything. Can we understand things the way they do? But it's true that if there's one good thing that Bhagoban has done, practically the only good thing in his life, it is to have his son admitted to a missionary school. He will be educated now. He will learn to think clearly. He will understand what is happening and why. Surely he will not be a blockhead like Bhagoban.

Porimal resumes pacing up and down in the corridor. The workers from the kitchen bring their dinner after a while. Ruti, dal, torkari. Dinner is served before sundown in all jails. The rules stipulate that prisoners must eat, wash their dishes and be locked up while daylight lasts. But the inmates of the cells are given a bit of leeway. They are allowed to keep their food and eat it later at night.

Having distributed the food amongst the wards, the kitchen workers have now come to the cells. From here they will go to the hospital. And then back to the chauka. The young man serving the rutis picks up a wad of four and thumps them down on Porimal's plate. Nobody except he and Porimal know of the note below the first two rutis. The long-awaited note has come from the comrades in Ward No. 7.

SEVEN

It is the deep of night. Darkness clings to the jail everywhere. The gong at the gate has just sounded the hour. But still Ashutosh Mandol cannot sleep. His blood is coursing through his veins in anticipation. Not much longer. This unbearably black night will end soon. The message has come from friends outside through secret channels. We're ready. If you have made adequate preparations, inform us of the day and time and the details of your plan.

The letters that come from the outside world go to the cells via Ward No. 7. From there to Ward No. 10. They are written in code. Other prisoners are unable to decipher them. An audacious plan is being drafted through the messages exchanged in the letters. Unless there is a debacle of some kind, it won't be long before an event that will shock the nation takes place.

The friends outside are desperate now. They are determined to free their comrades from the iron precincts of the jail. The letters hold their vow. No matter if the obstacles are insurmountable, we will let loose a river of blood if we can. They're capable of doing it, too. The entire country knows that they're pouring the hot bubbling blood in their veins into mills and factories, streets and bylanes, police stations and jails. They have refused to accept defeat.

Because of the strict surveillance of Naxals in the jail, it is impossible to gather all the comrades together to chalk out the plan. The enemy will be warned. So conversations take place between individuals only. Only after two people have agreed on an aspect of the plan is a third brought in to pass it on to a fourth.

But informing everyone of every detail of the plan is not the practice. This is revolutionary prudence. There may be a spy around. If there are supporters of Naxals among the guards, the other kind may exist too. So every individual knows only as much as he must know. Each one is supposed to fulfill the responsibility allotted to him with unquestioning loyalty. The entire plan will be at the fingertips of just three or four leaders, so that even if some parts are leaked, the whole thing will not fall apart.

Ashu Mandol belongs to a family which farms on a medium-sized plot of land. Thanks to farmland measuring some three acres, no one in the family has ever starved. He was a very bright student in school, always topping his class. His father had wanted him to go to college and be a doctor, but the son gave it all up to devote himself to fulfilling his dream of organising a peasants' revolution. Father and son had a bitter row over this. 'I'm a farmer myself,' Abhiram Mandol had said. 'I am no less aware than you of the suffering of farmers in the villages. You're mistaken if you think you know more than anyone else just because you've read two pages of a book. I fought in the Tebhaga uprising, I have faced untold suffering. Even today I believe that the plight of the people will not end till there is a revolution. But who's going to do it? The revolution is not some magic act that you can accomplish by waving a wand. People at large must be educated politically before a revolution can take place. There can be no revolution without educated and aware people. But where are these sensitive people who will plunge into the movement, staking all that they have? Everyone is throwing themselves at astrologers and god and gurus and political leaders in the hope of some crumbs. Is any of them standing up to the system with the determination to carve out their own destiny? That is why I believe people need to suffer even more. More starvation, more humiliation, more oppression. Only then will the wall of their forbearance finally crumble.

'You may say it's the age of revolution, that the entire nation is reeling from the labour pain of giving birth to a new society. But I think this is an unrealistic analysis. India is a huge country. So many languages, foods, clothes, mentalities. So many problems. The greatest of which is caste. All the poor and oppressed people have been fragmented into a thousand factions over thousands of years. Each of them is fighting for control of their own little fragments. And the enemies are applauding from a distance. They don't want the poor to unite. Nor do the poor themselves.

'Before there can be an agricultural revolution, or any of those other revolutions, I feel there has to be a social revolution. So that all the religions and communities and castes that come in the way of unity among people are ground to dust. Communists had raised this hope once upon a time. That was back during the Tebhaga movement. The Hindu, the Muslim, the Hanri, the Much, the Dom, the Lodh, the Koirborto – everyone ate together, lived together, fought shoulder to shoulder. But then the battle ended, the fox went back into its hole. Look at the farce – the powerful communist leader declares in his speech to the masses that no one is superior or inferior, and then goes home to organise his son's upanayan ceremony. Drapes a thread around his son's body and neck. What is this thread? An advertisement. Look, this thread says I'm high caste. Until this caste business ends and people become one, no revolution can succeed.

'Don't let this demon haunt you, Ashu. Study hard. I'll sell my land if needs be, to make sure you can go on studying. If you become a doctor, people of all castes will come to you. You can help them. People listen to those who help them. You can explain things to them then. Yes, this is a long drawn-out affair, it takes time to get results. It's like eggs. They have all the ingredients for creating a full life, but nothing can be rushed, and the mother hen knows this. She incubates the egg patiently for a long time. And her work doesn't end with the chick being hatched. She protects it, makes sure the hawk doesn't snatch it away. This is the way of nature. Nothing can change it. If you defy this and take the contrarian route, the outcome will be contrary too.'

Abhiram Mandol was not a highly educated man. But he had spent a lot of time in the company of educated people. He had gathered many experiences, which he used to analyse problems. Although actively involved in politics at one time, he had detached himself subsequently. A young Ashu had not been able to follow Abhiram's argument. He had felt that his father's perspective was the other side of the mirror. What lay at the root of the violence, the fissures, the discord among people was scarcity and the lack of education and awareness. Why would anyone resort to violence with their fellow men if they had enough to eat, if there was health and education for everyone? Everyone would be on the same level once economic disparities were removed, once there were no class differences in society. For this, the revolution had to be undertaken as quickly as possible. People no longer wanted advice, they wanted work. For thousands of years, from the Vedas to Karl Marx, the pundits had only dispensed sage counsel and inspirational messages. None of them had acted. It was time for action. How could the useful be told apart from the ineffective until they actually got down to doing things? If they made mistakes, those would have to be corrected. If the objective was clear, if no evil was intended, there was no harm in accepting errors. Dialectical arguments about which came first, the chicken or the egg, were nothing but distractions. There was just one goal now, one song: hit the road my friend, we will learn the way as we march on it. No more delays, my friend. Answer now, you must decide which path you want to take. Will you march with us and lend us your strength, or will you shout that we must be thwarted? The revolution will not stop, no matter how many blows the enemy strikes in desperation...

And so Ashu had destroyed his father's hopes as well as his own promising future by slitting a rich landowner's throat. What they called khatam. What was khatam? A wealthy individual's social, political and economic influence.

Ashu had been arrested for this crime. He is still on trial. Given the testimony of witnesses, he might even get the death sentence. Ashu is a valuable comrade for his party. His friends have vowed to shed their blood to free him.

Not for the past few days alone, but for a long time now, Ashu has been taking his fellow inmates aside one by one to ask, 'Are you mentally prepared to take part in a jailbreak? Tomorrow if not today, or the day after, or some time in the future. If you aren't, make your preparations at once. Because it is about to happen. I cannot tell you how it will be done, but there is no doubt that it will be done. You will get a few minutes' notice, but that's all. You'll have a minute at most to escape and then put at least two hundred metres between yourself and the jail. If you can do that, a vehicle will be waiting, arranged by our comrades outside, to take you away to a safe place. Two others and I will open the main gate. I cannot disclose their identities right now. It isn't even necessary. But you can trust us to get the gate opened. None of you must leave your wards in advance. Only after you see us opening the gate must you go in that direction, not a minute before. If you have any suggestions, tell us now. Everything will be planned meticulously and our comrades outside, informed accordingly.'

Kalyan had said, 'No, I have no suggestions. All I want to know is, why has 7 AM been chosen as the time? Is there a specific reason?'

'We have not chosen 7 AM. The time has not yet been finalised. But our friends outside have proposed that hour. The guards on night duty are back in their barracks at that time, and those who are not on morning duty are still in bed. So security is at its loosest then. After the tense vigil of the night, everyone relaxes a little. Another reason is that roads are relatively uncluttered at that hour. The traffic increases later in the day and there's often a jam at the gate. If our vehicles get stuck in that case, we will not be able to escape.'

'But we won't have any excuse to gather at the gate at 7 AM. If it's between two and two-thirty in the afternoon, the roads are relatively empty then as well. That's when people come to meet the prisoners; it's interview time. If we get visitors, preferably women, we will have a pretext to be there at the gate. As usual, the visitors will pass us cigarettes or something through the guard after the meeting. We will be near the wooden gate on this side of the main iron gate. As soon as the guard unlocks the wooden gate to give us the cigarettes, we can pounce on him and snatch the keys to the main gate.'

Ashu had had to accept Kalyan's reasoning. A previous attempt at jailbreak had failed when Porimal and some others had been unable to attack the guard as planned. They had a court appearance that day, from where they had smuggled arms into the jail. After the police van had deposited them inside, the deputy jailer was supposed to have them searched and then enter their names in the register. But the prisoners had attacked before this could be done. But the guard on duty at the gate had responded cleverly, tossing the keys through the bars of the gate to where they could not be reached. Thwarted, Porimal and the rest had changed their tactics, picking up the large metal weights used to weigh supplies and dashing them against the lock. After four or five blows, they had even managed to break the lock and open the gate, but it was too late by then. All the guards had come running from the barracks.

That mistake was not going to be repeated. Anyone who tried to approach the gate from the barracks would have to brave a barrage of bombs and gunfire. And if the guard on duty at the gate was attacked on the inner side of the wooden gate, he would not have the opportunity to toss the keys away.

'Not a bad idea,' said Ashu. 'This is worth thinking about. But the success of our plan depends on just one thing. Which is a weapon. We cannot achieve anything without arms. How do you suggest we get weapons into the jail?'

'Tell me what you're thinking.'

'You, I, Bhanu, Taposh – more or less everyone has court appearances in the next ten days. The fellow who brings our food and tea is now one of us. He will slip in a weapon with our food.'

'But how will you evade scrutiny at the gate to get it into the jail in the first place?'

'We can't do it when we're returning from the court, but we can do it later.'

'How?'

'You must have noticed the two large cupboards standing on our right when we line up in the deputy jailer's office. The space beneath them is filled with scraps of paper, which proves that it is never cleaned. The sweeper runs his brooms over the floor in front of the cupboard but never under them. Those of us who will bring back arms will quietly slip them beneath the cupboards. The entire jail is thoroughly searched once a month, the wards with the Naxals in particular. But once a search has been conducted, there's nothing to worry about for thirty days. The arms can stay safely beneath the cupboards. The deputy jailer's office is beyond suspicion in any case.'

Ashu had laughed. But Kalyan wasn't convinced. 'But how will the guns be fetched from the deputy jailer's office? Who will do it?'

'Is it essential to reveal names?' Ashu laughed again. 'Why don't you try to guess who it will be. This is why comrade Sudhangshu-da used to tell us: keep your faith in the people. Never doubt them. The people want a revolution. They're friends of the revolutionaries, their soulmates. They may mistakenly oppose the revolution for a short while, but the resistance isn't permanent. The one who will bring us the arms, or will stash them away somewhere else if he can't send them to us immediately, is Bashu.'

'But he's a chamcha, he's the authorities' man.'

'I used to think so too. But that's not the case. Bashu is very sympathetic to our cause. I spoke to him about doing this only after I was convinced. He's agreed.'

'Are you sure he won't betray us?'

'I am. But what can happen in his case can happen with you or me too – getting caught because of carelessness. Which is why no one else will talk to him about this. If he does get caught and is tortured, the only name he can reveal should be mine.'

Smiling, Ashu continued, 'Anyway, my chances of hanging are almost a hundred per cent. The only option for survival is to escape from jail. Nothing worse than death can come my way if the plan is divulged. So it's all right if Bashu comes to know my name. Let him assume I'm the only one involved in this plan. That's best for everyone.'

'Does he know about the jailbreak?'

'I haven't told him. But he may have guessed.'

Ashu's conversation with Kalyan had ended there. Taposh had brought up a different possibility. 'Suppose we're unable to snatch the keys for some reason. What will happen then? We'll all be killed like rats in a trap.' Ashu had pondered over this for quite a few days. Yes, there had to be a fallback plan. There would be no chance to improvise once the action began. Only two outcomes were possible then: victory or death. 'This is absolutely true. Things may not turn out the way we're planning them.' Taposh was right. 'What should we do if we're unable to get hold of the keys?'

After much thought, Ashu had a glimmer of an idea. It wouldn't enable all the prisoners to escape, however. If they could grab the keys, not only would the Naxals rush out like floodwater, many of the other prisoners wouldn't waste the opportunity either. But the second option would allow no more than a dozen to escape. Just a dozen out of so many – far too small a number.

A tall ladder lay in the field next to amdani. Electricians used it to fix new wires, repair old ones, and replace the lights. No one was allowed into that part of the field. The authorities were not worried about it since the area was within range of the rifles with which sentries manned the watchtower.

Ashu decided that if it came to that, the ladder could be propped up against the wall, allowing some people to scale the wall and jump into the fetid waters of the canal running behind it. They would have to wade or swim across to the other side and lose themselves in the crowd there. It would be no small feat if even one person could escape instead of everyone being killed. There would be loss of lives, but this was only in case the main gate couldn't be opened. And the main gate would certainly be opened.

However, it isn't this eventuality but something else that has Ashu worried right now. The moment the main gates are opened, it won't be just the Naxals but also the opportunists among the other prisoners who will make a run for it. And every guard in every corner of the jail will give chase. Although it will be only eleven or twelve of them at first, within thirty seconds their numbers will swell to twenty-six. These twenty-six guards will have to be stopped at the case-table until the prisoners have escaped. Who's going to take that responsibility? Whoever does will have no way to escape himself. While the rest will have at least a fifty per cent chance of survival, this person will face certain death. Who will take this responsibility knowingly? Who will be ready to lay down his life? This is making him fret. It's not something anyone can be requested to do. The only possibility is to do it himself. Ashu has no regret about that. If someone else takes the responsibility for unlocking the gate, he will take his position by the case-table with a gun and keep the prison guards at bay. If the murderous group of twenty-six guards still want to advance towards the gate, they will have to do it over his dead body.

Ashu must discuss this with his comrades. His friends outside, especially those who are risking their own lives to implement this audacious plan, will be disappointed. He must not let them know that he will not be escaping. There's no need to dash their hopes. Everyone's life is important, there's no difference in value. How can you push another person into the flames? It's better to offer yourself for sacrifice. At least he will not have to consider himself a selfish coward. But the proposal will need everyone's approval. And someone else will have to take the responsibility of unlocking the main gate.

Now he must write a short note and send it to the cells. Ashu draws a pen and a sheet of paper to himself.

EIGHT

It is still the dead of night. A lifeless light is spread out across the jail. There's no sound anywhere. The large buildings are as silent as tombs. Young Sukumar Singh, the guard on duty at the hospital, is fed up. He cannot stand the mosquitoes, the darkness, the loneliness anymore. He feels like doing something disruptive.

As a young boy Sukumar was very mischievous. No one could match him when it came to inventing pranks. Once, he had tied crackers to a dog's tail and set them off. Terrified out of its wits, the dog had raced off and plunged into a bale of hay, which went up in flames. Sukumar's father had thrashed him within an inch of his life.

Not that this reformed him. His mother was dead, and his father had married again. His stepmother may have stepped out of the kitchen for a minute, Sukumar would swiftly drop a fistful of salt into the vegetables and go back to chanting the tables. He would savour the beating she received at his father's hand when the food was served. He was a storehouse of destructive ideas. His stepmother and little stepbrother might be sleeping on a mat near the door in the afternoon, Sukumar would silently release a bunch of red ants near them and run away.

Even as a grown-up, he has not given up the habit of troubling others, harassing his colleagues whenever possible. Just the other day, a guard on duty at the wall had slid into a sitting position and dozed off. Sukumar stole his stick surreptitiously and hid it. This is what jailers do. When they go on their rounds at night, if they see anyone sleeping on the job, they take away their cap or stick, demanding to see the missing object the next day. Sometimes they even issue show-cause notices for dereliction of duty.

The guard was distraught when he woke up and couldn't find his stick. That was when Sukumar produced it with a wide smile, earning some choice expletives in the process.

Now he wants to do some mischief here in the dark. Something that will not only energise his flagging spirits but also help pass the time. But what can he do? Wait, how about dressing up as Bandiswala? After all, Bandiswala is often seen walking around the jail, screaming. Who is it really? Obviously one of the guards dressed up as Bandiswala. Then why not me tonight, he thinks.

No sooner does the idea occur to him than he reaches out between the bars of a hospital window with his stick to snag a large white sheet. All the sheets and towels, as well as the prisoners' uniforms, are milk white. If he wraps them around himself, no one can tell from a distance whether they're garments or bandages. In any case, the colour white is a symbol of dread in this jail after dark. Everyone turns pale with fear at the thought of dressing in white. R N Dutta, the security officer, likes to wear a white shirt and white trousers. One night, he was sneaking into the jail to check on the guards. The sentry on duty at the case-table did not realise that the officer had crept up behind him. Happening to look over his shoulder, he discovered a terror in white and fainted on the spot. R N Dutta does not dress in white anymore when visiting the jail at night.

Now Sukumar Singh wraps his face and head in a white sheet like dacoits did in the old days. Then he walks along the path leading away from the hospital towards the chauka. This spot is particularly dark because of the trees here, especially the banyan tree. The guard on duty at the chauka has his eyes shut. Picking up a lump of coal, Sukumar goes up to Ward No. 2 in silence. Then, standing on the steep staircase on which Lachman Singh had been burnt alive by the boiling gruel, Sukumar screams grotesquely, 'Jal gaya, I'm burning!' The scream echoes horribly, bouncing off every wall of every building. The echoes are accompanied by the terrorised shouts of people. Now Sukumar races up to the middle of the jail and flings the lump of coal in his hand into the pond. It sounds as though Bandiswala has jumped into the water. Then he runs back to the hospital, tosses the white sheet back inside through the bars, and sits there with an innocent expression. Things have turned out exactly as he had wanted. Just as they had when he had set the dog's tail on fire with crackers. The entire jail is trembling with fright.

The jailer and the deputy jailer get an account of the night's events in their office the next morning. Taking a pinch of snuff, the deputy jailer says, 'He hasn't shown himself for some time. I wonder what's brought him back suddenly. Some rule must have been broken somewhere in the jail. How will I spend the rest of my years here? It's not possible to deal with all these ghosts, spirits and demons. You have to do something, Jailer-babu. Otherwise something catastrophic may happen...'

'What can I do?' the jailer asks hopelessly. 'This is not for ojhas or gunins. I don't think witch doctors or exorcists can solve this.'

'My gurudeb is not some ojha or witch doctor. He's a tantric sage. He's been perfecting and purifying himself for twelve years at Kamrup Kamakhya. I don't know if you'll believe me, but he can start a fire just by uttering a mantra.'

'Nothing difficult about that.'

'What do you mean! Not difficult?'

'You can learn the trick yourself from any ordinary book on magic.'

'You're equating tantra with magic,' the deputy jailer says, in a voice laden with sadness. 'There's nothing more I can say.'

Lowering his head, he begins to make notations in the register. Jotting down the names of the prisoners who have court appearances scheduled, he passes them to Paresh the 'writer', saying, 'Make sure they're here on time.' The jailer realises that his deputy is hurt. It is wrong to attack someone's faith. It is also a crime according to the Constitution. To atone for his mistake, the jailer says, 'Deputy-babu, do you think we can be delivered from this danger if we conduct a ceremonial joggo with priests and a fire?'

'Of course we can,' answers his deputy. 'Stones used to rain down on the roof of one of the houses in our neighbourhood every night. The infestation has stopped after gurudeb performed a ritual.'

The jailer wants to say that this was not the work of spirits, that neighbourhood louts often throw stones at houses where young women live. Sometimes the pebbles are accompanied by letters. This usually takes place in areas with mixed populations or in refugee colonies. Such incidents are never seen in posh localities. Why not? Because such methods of harassing young women are unknown in those areas... Instead, he says, 'Weren't you saying the suppliers would pay for all this? But why should they pay, considering the problem is ours?'

Deputy Jailer Mohinimohon-babu grins. 'Very simple. You have to invest for returns. They're businessmen, clever people. They want us under their thumb.'

'But they already have us under their thumb. When the IG and the Superintendent are like puppets in their hands, who are we to mutiny? Has anyone ever survived after displeasing the boss?'

'That's true,' stammers the deputy, 'but then Pagla Daktar loses his head at times. There was a huge scene over the chinre just before you were posted here, and then he rejected a quintal of fish supplied by the contractor. Everyone's been on tenterhooks since then, especially the fish and meat suppliers.

Pagla Daktar might beat them up if they offer him money directly. A bit Naxal-minded, you see. Very scrupulous. Never ready to bend the laws. Which is why he hasn't got anywhere. Doesn't have a house of his own even after twenty-five years of work. Still lives in a rented flat.'

Jailer Bireshwar Mukherjee smiles. 'So they want to use the Bandiswala case to bribe the doctor, you and me through this ritual. Excellent. It's wise to have an illness treated. A grand ceremony, all of us present with our families, treats for everyone. Good idea!'

The warehouse clerk, Shurjo-babu, short and plump, rushes in. His face is red with agitation, and sweat is dripping from his body. Throwing himself into a chair, he pants loudly. Giving him a little time to recover, the jailer says, 'What's the matter?'

'I was that close to being killed. Escaped by the skin of my teeth. How would I have known... My god, the entire station is awash with blood! Nine or ten dead, I'm sure.'

'Where? Who's dead?'

'GRP Force. Naxal attack on the camp at dawn. They were all asleep. No scope for resistance. Escaped with five rifles. I got out of the train bang in the middle of it all. Can't stop trembling now. Ghastly!'

Shurjo-babu drains a glass of water, wiping his perspiration with the back of his hand. 'This place is turning into hell,' he continues. 'Who knows when we'll be released from all this. Can't take it anymore. Bombs-guns-daggers everywhere. And people keep getting killed...'

'Best not to hope for release,' says the deputy jailer. 'Between Naxals and Bandiswala, we've got our backs to the wall. He was seen again last night.'

'I wish I could quit this job and run away,' says Shurjo-babu. 'But run away where? There's nowhere to live in peace. Kakdwip, Sundarban, Bankura, Purulia – nowhere. All in flames.'

The doctor arrives. He's perpetually busy with something or the other. Today he's in a foul temper, no one knows why. Muttering to himself, he enters through the gate and appears in front of the office. The guard will unlock the iron gate here, let him through, close it behind him, and only then unlock the wooden gate for him. He doesn't have the patience for all this. He's chafing. 'Open up, Sukhdev. Quickly! The boy had a hundred and two fever last night. Hundred and two. Who knows how he is now. Not a drop of medicine anywhere. How am I supposed to treat him? How am I supposed to treat him without medicines? If there are no medicines, what am I doing here? What am I doing here? Breathing the same air as the doctor doesn't cure anyone. You need medicines to treat illnesses. Nothing, we have nothing.'

'I'm still trembling,' Shurjo-babu says after the doctor leaves.

'You work in a jail,' the deputy jailer scolds him. 'How can you be so squeamish about shooting and blood?'

'No, it's just that I was caught in the middle of it. The train had just stopped. In that crowd... I could have easily... Very lucky, I must say.'

'Enough of news of the world, now let me give you some news from the jail. He has been seen again.'

'When?'

'Last night.'

'My god!'

The jailer, deputy jailer and Shurjo-babu exchange glances. They have no idea what to say or do now.

NINE

The much-awaited Saturday with its zero hour is here. The day when the outcome of long days of planning will be known. All preparations have been completed. Two revolvers have arrived at the jail from the courts in two installments. Having spent the night beneath the deputy jailer's cupboard, they have reached Ward No. 7, tucked discreetly at Bashu's waist. Word has been sent to the people outside the jail who matter. The time of the operation is between two and two-thirty in the afternoon. As they leave after meeting the prisoners to gather all the last minute news, Kallol-da, Purobi-di and Jayashree will send the signal to the friends waiting outside.

A group of people from the party will be watching out for the signal. As soon as they get it, they will split into two, one of them advancing towards the police barracks and the other taking up position on the road just outside the jail gate. They will keep an eye on the main iron gate within. The moment Porimal and the rest open it, this group will attack the guard stationed on the road with guns and bombs. When they hear the sounds of this attack, the other group will keep hurling bombs at the police barracks so that no one can come out to help the jail guards.

The police barracks are at the northern end of the jail. At the southern end, a third group of people will be waiting with a number of taxis at different points on the road. They will threaten the drivers with their gun, snatch the keys, and drive the vehicles as close to the main gate as possible, so that their comrades who have just escaped from prison can jump in quickly.

The planning is flawless. Now it's just a matter of waiting for the right time. Ashu has woken up at the crack of dawn. Not that he, or most of the others, have slept much at night. Their eyes are red, their breathing already laboured. Their hearts are thumping. They're not talking much amongst themselves. Everyone is going about their daily tasks mechanically.

The sun cannot be seen rising from Ward No. 7. Ward No. 1 comes in the way. It is visible only after 8 AM. The jailer's morning round and breakfast are over by then.

Ashu hasn't been able to focus on his breakfast today. Nor has anyone who knows that today is the day. Those who don't will be informed a little later, when they are called for their meetings with visitors by the 'writer' Paresh.

At eight, Ashu spots the sun blazing above Ward No. 1. A fiery, angry sun. As though it's bleeding from every pore in its body. As the sun climbs, the tumult in Ashu's heart reaches a crescendo.

It's the same inside the cell. All five of them know what is to take place shortly. These are old comrades who have been tested before. Their integrity has been proven time and again when they have walked through fire. So no detail of the blueprint has been kept from them. It is not yet known whether every prisoner in the Naxal ward is as militant and unwavering in their ideology.

One of these others is named Samaresh. His brother is a leader in a different political party. There is news that he is trying to furnish a bond with his brother's help so that he can get out of jail. He joined the Naxals only a few months ago. The police had found nothing more than a copy of Mao's Red Book and a few copies of the Naxalite mouthpiece Deshbroti when arresting him. There is no serious allegation against him. Apparently he has told the police that he joined the Naxals under threats. He has been in jail for just two months, and is hoping to be freed in another two. Informing him of such a crucial plan was out of the question. There was no assurance of his participation. He might even sabotage the effort. So he hasn't been told anything, and he won't be told, either.

There's another young man named Borun. Afraid of being tortured, he has revealed the address of a secret lair of the party to the police. Although the police was not able to arrest anyone there, they found some expensive weapons procured with great effort. Apparently the police have offered to withdraw their case against him and get him a job with the Home Guard if he can spy on the Naxals in jail and pass on the information.

Who knows, spreading these rumours might also be a secret strategy of Deputy Commissioner Gupta's, meant to sow the seeds of suspicion between the Naxals in jail and destroy their unity. Because Borun still claims he did not confess anything to the police.

In jail it isn't possible to know for sure what's going on outside. Mihir, who was arrested a few days after Borun, has been supplying news of what's been happening out there.

Still, no one about whom there is the slightest of suspicion has been told anything in advance. They will be told as soon as Porimol, Ashu and Kalyan open the gates.

A few trusted comrades will be watching the gate through the windows of Ward No. 7. They will also be listening closely. As soon as they hear the explosions of bombs, all of them will rush in unison towards the gate. Some of them will ask their cellmates to join them. There's no harm if they don't, either. Bijon, Nemai, Goutam and Bablu will be waiting. The moment they hear the others running, they will climb on the water tank from the veranda outside their cells, jump from there to the toilet roof, and then leap to the ground to race towards the gate past the case-table.

All of this cannot possibly take place peacefully. The guards on duty at the cells and at Ward No. 2 are bound to stop them. They will blow on their whistles to summon reinforcements. And the twenty-six guards stationed at different points in the jail are certain to charge at them together. There is no other route to the jail gate. The guards will have to be stopped right here, so that they can go no further till all the comrades have escaped.

The problem is, who's going to take on this responsibility? Everyone else will get away, but the person preventing the guards from advancing will have to remain here. Not just that, the violence that will follow the jailbreak is almost guaranteed to lead to this person's death. Which of the prisoners here will die willingly?

Ashu had said, 'I can stay back if someone else can take the responsibility of opening the gate. I think that's the right thing for me to do. Or else later. By later I don't mean tomorrow, but when the history of these events is written, my role might be considered insignificant, even selfish. Everyone has to die some day, after all. Maybe today, maybe a hundred years later. I don't want anyone to smear my name with disrepute. So I really want to be in charge of the resistance here.'

A letter went to Ashu from his fellow-conspirators, severely criticizing his idea. 'It's all very well to be emotional, but that cannot be allowed to overrule reason. You want to sacrifice your life. The foundations of our party are built on the great tradition of sacrifice. Thousands of comrades have maintained, and continue to maintain, that tradition with their own blood. There's nothing new about it. Comrade Mao has said, wherever there is injustice, there is resistance, and death is a daily occurrence there.

'We will have to sacrifice someone's life here. Since it cannot be avoided at any cost, it will be done. But it can never be yours, no matter how stricken you are at the thought of how you will be judged by history. The task of a revolutionary is to live and die for the revolution. History is a minor matter.

'Our comrades outside consider you extremely important at this point of time. If you can lend your support to the valiant peasants fighting in the villages and dreaming of creating free zones, they will be more inspired. You must get out of jail specifically for the sake of the people who have suffered untold miseries. The need is not yours as much as it is the party's.

'Therefore you are going. We, your comrades in the cell, will take the responsibility for resisting the guards. The identity of the person who will be given the task is currently under discussion. You will be informed later.'

After this, the deliberations in the cells had gathered pace. It was no longer limited to an exchange of notes. They had sat down around a ludo board in front of Cell No. 1, out of sight of anyone passing outside.

Bhojon Biswas was on duty at the cells. He carried a thick stick like everyone else, but he didn't even scold anyone unless absolutely necessary, leave alone use his stick. The deputy jailer mocked him for this reason, saying, 'Sticks don't suit you, Bhojon, carry a flute instead. Play a melody for the prisoners to win their hearts.'

Bhojon avoids confrontations. He does not speak harshly to anyone, be it a prisoner or another guard. In appearance he is plain, utterly nondescript, in fact. His eyes signal a deep-seated sorrow that he carries within him. And because he cannot share the burden with anyone else, his anguish grows heavier by the day.

'Tell me, Bhojon-da, why did you take this job?' Nemai had asked him one day. 'No one can do a job well if it does not give them joy. You don't look like your heart is in this work. Why did you choose to do it then?'

'What makes you think my heart is not in it. This job feeds me. How can I be indifferent to the source of my livelihood?'

'You're not saying this from your heart, you're just mouthing the words. There are seventy-seven other guards, but you're different from all of them. All of them turn up for duty with large bags, they're constantly looking for things they can steal. I never see you doing anything like that.'

'To each his own.'

'That's why I'm asking you, why don't you do what they do?'

Bhojon Biswas was no longer on duty at the jail. His mind and heart had broken through the walls and gates to fly to a tiny home in an unknown corner of a Bengal village. Where his small family used to live. He remembered his son.

'There are many things I cannot do,' he said. 'Not everyone can follow the crowd. I am among the few who can't. I'm fine this way. I may go hungry to bed, I may be poor, but I live honestly and in happiness. My son says, anything you do that you regret afterwards is wrong. And the things you do that let you hold your head high is right. There's no such thing as divine sin or divine virtue or heaven or hell. Suppose you do something that tears you apart with anguish. Is that not a hellish torment? Everyone makes mistakes. Taking this job was a mistake. But never do something that is wrong, that is unjust. This is what my son says.'

'How many sons do you have?'

'Just the one. It was when giving birth to him that...' Bhojon broke off, looking up wistfully at the sky. Nemai doesn't ask any more questions. He has understood.

A twenty-two-year-old Bhojon and an eighteen-year-old Shondhya had been married according to village rituals, as Bhojon's father had wanted. He had been very keen on a grandson, but twelve years passed without his desire being met. Both of Bhojon's parents died. Many of his neighbours suggested marrying again. A son was essential to preserve the family line. What else could he do, since his wife was barren. But Bhojon paid no heed. He loved his wife deeply. He couldn't bring himself to do anything that would hurt her.

Finally, just when everyone had given up hope, Shondhya got pregnant. And then, while giving birth, she developed an infection in her cervix. Rural medical facilities were hopeless. Shondhya's life could not be saved. She died after several days of suffering. Bhojon's happiness went up in flames on Shondhya's pyre.

But bringing up his son was a problem. Bhojon had no choice but to remarry. But his new wife could neither bring herself to love Bhojon and his son, nor consider them her own husband and child. After making their lives miserable for five years, she ran away with a young man from the neighbourhood.

Bhojon's son Pujon reached school-going age. He had no way to have his son live with him. He was transferred often, so he had to get his son admitted to a boarding school. Bhojon had no control over how the boy was growing up. He had been promoted to class nine last year, after which he had run away from school.

When he met Bhojon, he said, 'It's all rubbish. They're

making us memorise a bunch of wrong facts and plain lies. If this is education, I don't want any of it...'

Bhojon looked at his son in wonder. A lanky, rather thin boy, with the first faint signs of adulthood on his chin. Innocent, unwavering, wide eyes. Such a loveable boy... And then a suddenly grown-up Pujon, who appeared just a little bit unfamiliar. He said, 'Baba, this education system was set up by the British for the people of this country to be their servants, so that we consider slavery honourable. The British have left, but the educational system has not changed. Look at the number of fine young boys and girls studying madly day and night. But to what end? To get a job. To serve. Which is what servants to. And this service has been glorified so much that everyone believes securing a job is the ultimate achievement of life.

'See how strange it is, Baba. The people who toil the hardest in our country are the farmers. Their blood, sweat and tears give us our golden harvests. But they earn so little in comparison to their labour that they can barely feed themselves.

'Take a factory worker, whose hands have created our civilization, without whom development is impossible. Leave alone paying him fair wages, society doesn't even acknowledge him as the maker of those products. Chasha-mojur is a derogatory term. The farmer and the labourer are the lowest of the low.

'Our education stuffs just one idea into students' heads. You're educated. There's no honour for an educated person in working as a labourer or tilling the soil. Only a job will ensure your status. The more of a servant you are, the greater your salary and social standing. I'm not willing to sweat over my books day and night to become someone's servant, Baba.'

'What do you want to do for a living then?'

'I'm thinking about it. Let's see.'

Bhojon was saddened when his son dropped out of school, but he couldn't be angry. There was truth in what Pujon had said. Mahim Joardar, who lived nearby, was a farmer. He had sold his land to finance his son's career in Calcutta. The boy got himself a law degree, and eventually refused to acknowledge his father who was a farmer. Mohim had apparently been humiliated in Calcutta when he went to visit his son, who had saved face in front of his friends by introducing his father as a farm-hand back home.

But even if he wasn't angry, Bhojon was afraid. It was not the best of times. Young people were seething with rage. There was scarcity everywhere. No one was calm these days. What if his son fell in with such people? But his one hope lay in the fact that Pujon was not an angry young man. He was quiet, restrained, reserved. And his greatest quality was that he was a singer. He wrote his own songs. During the floods, he had composed songs about the disaster, and travelled around like a minstrel, performing them and collecting money to send to the affected areas.

The last time Bhojon went home on a week's leave, he did not meet his son. A distant cousin said he had seen Pujon, along with two or three others like him, wandering around in Hatkhola village.

Hatkhola was a long way away. Why was Pujon in Hatkhola, whom was he meeting there, for what purpose? Bhojon had not had any peace of mind ever since his return to Calcutta. He was in a constant state of worry. He had written to Pujon repeatedly but received no reply. He needed to go home again. But the new jailer was refusing him leave. Apparently some unrest was brewing here in the jail. It was essential for every one on the staff to be present in full strength.

Miserable and weighed down with misgivings, Bhojon Biswas was seated in front of the cell, leaning against the wall, lost in thought, while Porimol, Bijon and the rest were hunched over a ludo board, discussing their tactics.

Arranging the pieces on the board, Porimal said in a low, steady voice, 'By my reckoning, I should be given the responsibility to hold the guards. We don't have unlimited arms. Just the one revolver. Six bullets for twenty-six guards. They must be allowed to come very close. Firing from point-blank range will injure two or three of them and stop the rest in their tracks. All of you know how good my aim is. No purpose will be served by getting nervous and firing at random. That's why I'm the one who needs to be here.'

Moving a red piece forward two places, Bijon said, 'But then who will perform the main task? The success of the mission depends on snatching the keys from the guard on duty at the gate. We have no idea who will be posted there. If it's that bullheaded Bihari muscleman Dhanpat, it won't be easy. Which of us can match up to him in physical strength? That's why you must be the one to grab the keys. I'll take up position here to resist the guards.'

Nemai jumped in immediately to thwart Bijon's plan. 'It won't be any of you, it'll be me. Comrade CM has said a communist who has not dipped his fingers in the class enemy's blood is no communist. I haven't done it yet, I'm not letting this chance go. I'll keep them at bay till everyone escapes. I don't care what happens to me after that.'

But Bablu and Goutam were not ready to give up their claim either. Everyone put up an argument in favour of themselves as the ideal candidate to resist the advancing guards. A faltu appeared suddenly with the afternoon tea. The discussion was postponed.

Dividing the tea into eight portions, one of them called out to Bhagoban. Unwell for a few days, he had been lying down in his own cell. Bijon had told the doctor of his illness, only to be scolded. 'What's the use of giving him medicine? What's the use of medicine? Can you tell me what purpose it'll serve? Let him go instead. Let him go. He's in jail all the time. A thief. Once a thief, always a thief. Won't be reformed. Keeps coming back to jail. Keeps coming back. No medicines in jail. Good people die without treatment. Jyotirmoy-babu in Ward No. 10. A comrade of yours. Bronchitis. No medicine. He's dying. What's the use of looking after thieves. What's the use. In jail, out in the world, just thieves everywhere.'

Bhagoban came out of his cell and sat down in the corridor, sipping a glass of tea. Handing a glass to the faltu, Goutam said,

'Give this to Bhojon-da.' Accepting it, Bhojon said hesitantly, 'It's not right for me to drink your tea every day. It's not easy for prisoners to get tea and sugar.'

'So what?'

'Nothing, I just feel strange. How long will you do it anyway?'

'Only as long as we're here. After that, who knows where we'll be?'

'What do you mean? Is there some talk of setting you free? Someone was saying all Naxals will be released unconditionally.'

'Who told you this, Bhojon-da? We've been hearing just the opposite. Naxals will be mopped up from all over the country. The military will be pressed into action if needs be.'

Bhojon sipped his tea. He seemed wrapped in thought. He said nothing. His eyes were on the sky again.

The faltu sipped his tea too. Then he set off for the tubewell. Six pitchers had to be filled with water. The prisoners locked into their cells mustn't die of thirst at night.

Draining his tea, Bhagoban suddenly told Porimal, 'Can you tell me what I'm worth in this world? Bolti paaro, kawto dam? How much? In jail or outside it, no one considers me a human being. What's the use of my staying alive?'

Porimol looked in surprise at this self-reflective Bhagoban. The others too felt uncomfortable at these questions. Bhagoban continued, 'My father used to steal things. Hunger made him a thief. I was very young. Wherever I went people called me a chorer chhabal. Son of a thief. I have a son. Studies in a missionary school. He'll grow up one day. He'll know what I'm like. How will he feel if people call him a chorer chhabal too?'

'He'll feel terrible,' Porimal said gently.

'You people are educated. Clever. Tell me some way... So that my son is not called the son of a thief. So that he doesn't have to hang his head in shame.'

'For that you'll have to give up all this and do something good, something that will earn you a name,' Porimal said. 'If your virtues are greater than your vices, the good will drown out the bad.'

'Taito boltichhi. That's what I'm saying. What should I do?'

'What should you do? How can we tell you?' Porimal was at a loss for words.

'I knew you wouldn't be able to tell me,' Bhagoban continued after a pause. 'Then let me tell you instead. You know when you were whispering just now? I heard every word. Ears of a thief. I can listen to a sleeping man breathing and know how deeply he's sleeping. What I'm saying is, the task that all of you are fighting over – give it to me. I'll hold them back, I won't let them catch you.'

It wasn't words but grenades that Bhagoban seemed to have lobbed into their hearts. How had he overheard them despite all the secrecy? Now what? Was everything going to collapse at the last minute? Would the mission fail?

'Deputy-babu sent me to this cell to spy on you,' Bhagoban continued. 'But after I started living here with all of you, talking to you, becoming one of you... I've grown fond of you. Bishom maya... You're such good people. Suffering so much.

For everyone else out there. You cannot sacrifice your lives for such a small task. All of you must get out. And do something good for the poor.'

Porimal stammered. His throat was dry, the words wouldn't leave his mouth. He was like a tree felled by lightning.

Still Bhagoban kept speaking. 'Don't imagine I'm doing it for you. I have something to gain too. After this, no son of a bitch will dare call me a chorer chhabal. Everyone will say Bhagoban Sardar was actually a Naxal. I've seen outside how they respect Naxals. My son won't be ashamed of his father anymore.'

Bhagoban was no actor. He did not know how to present a lie in the form of a truth. All that he had said had come from his heart, a blazing and determined vow. Leave alone mere mortals, even mountains part when faced with such an iron will.

TEN

After lunch the afternoon headcount is conducted according to routine. The jamadar leaves after locking the gates. Two hours to go. The gates will be unlocked again at exactly 2 PM. But not everyone will be allowed out. Venturing out without permission means taking the guards' sticks on your back. Only those who have meetings scheduled are permitted to leave their wards. All of them will gather at the case-table. They will be despatched in groups of ten to the rooms with the wire mesh, from where they will return with whatever their friends or relatives have brought them. Paresh the 'writer' has called out the names a short while ago. Kalyan, Ashu and Porimal have meetings scheduled with visitors. It's Saturday. Only political prisoners have meetings on Saturdays. There are many others who have meetings scheduled too, but none of them has an inkling of the plot. They have no idea that the most invincible fortress of the state machinery will be breached today. And that they will have a chance to flee, too, because of their proximity to the gate. Unless their senses take leave of them, they might be the first to be free.

Ashu takes Kalyan's hand. No words, just an intimate touch, in an effort to convey what cannot be said in words. Both their hands are trembling. Their blood cells are whipping up a storm in their arteries and veins. The slightest miscalculation, the smallest error, will endanger the lives of hundreds. No one knows which of them will survive, or who will die. They will be the ones to make the first move, to initiate the violent jailbreak. Whatever the outcome, the responsibility for it all – good or bad, successful or disastrous – lies on their shoulders. For many, many years, people will point at them to say – it was because of these three.

Ashu says, 'All lives are valuable. Not everyone who works at the jail as a guard is our enemy. Some are even friends who cannot be compared with anyone else. But they will also try to stop us, they have no choice. Try to ensure that no one is hurt unnecessarily. They too have parents and family and wives and children. Their tears should not be a cause for repentance for us afterwards.'

Kalyan nods. 'We'll try to use fear as a weapon to get our way. But there's nothing I can do if any of them is keen on getting a medal for bravery. This isn't a friendly match where we can win tomorrow even if we lose today. Here defeat means annihilation. So we have to try with all our might to win. Excessive kindness or compassion will spell danger for us. And besides, our opponents are fierce, they won't pardon us. What the Chairman says is right in these cases: keeping the enemy alive means death.'

'You're right,' says Ashu, 'but a revolutionary is not a murderer. The murderer only wants to kill. But a revolutionary must think of many things before taking a life.'

'The thinking can go on till the battle begins. There is no time for thought once it has started. There's only one task then: strike. Overwhelm the enemy with your attack. Win the battle.'

'Still, make an effort. No matter how dire the situation, don't let your heart turn to stone.'

Ashu is silent for a few minutes. He can recall his father's face. Stricken with grief and despair, Abhiram Mandol, an active communist now bent over with the weight of the world, had visited his son in jail a few times. Leaning his forehead on the wire mesh separating them, he had said, 'Maybe it would have been better for you to have become a doctor, to have got married and settled down, to have looked after your mother and me. You're our only son. Parents always have their expectations. But still, now I feel what you're doing is more important. Even if nothing else is achieved, at least the tyrants have been forced to retreat. People couldn't breathe earlier, now they can at least exhale. Perhaps nothing vital will be achieved. But this is important.'

'Don't feel sorry for me, Baba.'

'How can parents not feel sorry when their son is rotting in jail? I can still manage, but your mother... She won't live much longer. Her asthma is getting worse. Do they give parole here?'

In his head Ashu says, 'Forget parole, we're looking for full freedom. The time is coming. Either the executioner's noose or the policeman's bullet. And if the plan is successful, real freedom. That day is almost here.'

There are five young men in the cell. No, not five but six, one of whom is Bhagoban. He too is sailing on the high tide of young blood. He feels no regret or remorse, no fear or doubt. He knows that all's well that ends well. All the past evils will be buried today beneath a mountain of good. He had said, 'Look, all that begins must end. Whether you believe it or not, it will happen to me too one day. You read the papers, all of you. Don't you read about pickpockets and thieves being beaten to death by the public? What do they call it? Lynching. Gawnodholai. Bunch of people beat a man to death like he's a snake. That's the end I'll come to. It's how my father died. What's the use dying that way? I've got a chance now. I'll die from bullets instead. Blood spurting from my chest. Bholke bholke rawkto naambe. Blood to rinse all my sins and wrongdoings. Have any of you seen Rikta Nodir Baandh? I have. I forget his name, the dacoit. Looted so many people. Finally died for his countrymen. Everyone said he was great. Only those who die for other people go to heaven. I've forgotten the line after that.'

Paresh is heard at the cell door. 'Interview-wala, chalo. Come along, all those who have meetings.' Jail language. Casewala, courtwala, khanswala. There's a comparatively high proportion of Bihari Muslims here. Even the guards are mostly Hindi-speaking. So the main language in the jail is Hindi.

Porimal is ready. Going out of his cell, he looks at his four friends. Signals with his eyes. Bijon and Nemai understand what he's trying to say. Porimal follows Paresh towards the case-table. Kalyan and Ashu are there already. As they walk along, Porimal tells Paresh, 'Send Ashu, Kalyan and me together, all right? I can have a chat with them.'

'Ashu-da has told me already,' says Paresh.

'Who's on gate duty today, Paresh?' asks Porimal. 'Is it Bir Bahadur?'

'No, Bhojon-da's at the gate today.'

'Bhojon-da!' Porimal is surprised by the change. 'Why him? Doesn't the roster change every week?'

'Bir Bahadur fell ill suddenly.'

'Today of all days!'

'Why?' Paresh joked, 'How would having Bir Bahadur help? He likes thieves and dacoits equally, but he hates Naxals. Having Bhojon-da on duty is a thousand times better.'

'It's a question of timing. It would have been best not to have had Bhojon-da today. And to have had Bir Bahadur instead.'

About twenty people are gathered near the case-table. Ashu and Kalyan are among them. Ashu is armed. Kalyan and Porimal know this. The other gun is in the cell. Bhagoban has his hands on it by now. It has been given to him with the safety catch off. All he has to do is press the trigger with a steady hand.

Finally, Porimal and his companions are called. Paresh has sent them off together. The jail gate is a hundred yards away from the case-table. Beyond the gate on the other side are the wire-mesh rooms against the wall. The visitors are there already. Five or six feet of space separate the wire-mesh windows through which the visitor and the prisoner can see each other. A mother is sobbing at the appearance of her son.

'Why do you look this way? Don't they give you enough to eat? Don't hide anything from me.' A father is shouting at his son, 'It would have been better not to have had children than a bastard like you. You've ruined the family honour. Your Baro Mama rang, he said if you follow instructions, he'll find a way to have you released.'

Porimal can see Jayashree through the mesh. She's the same as always. No change in four years. The mole on her cheek is just as enticing. She still gets a dimple when she smiles. Her eyes still glow warmly. There's no time. This is not a moment for softness. Porimal conveys everything quickly. 'All well.' Kallol-da and Purobi-di get the same message from Ashu and Kalyan. 'All well.' They're a middle-aged couple. They present themselves as Ashu's uncle and Kalyan's sister, respectively, for the meeting with the prisoners. That was the instruction from the party. Someone younger would have been in danger. You never know when detectives are lying in ambush.

The two of them complete their conversation, deposit the food they had brought for the prisoners at the gate, and go back out on the road. One of them walks northward and the other, southward. Signalling to the young men loitering at the end of the road on both sides, they disappear in the crowd.

Jayashree, too, deposits her things and stops on the main road outside the jail gate, as though she's waiting for a bus. Her eyes are on the gate, however. It will be opened soon. Porimal will open it. She will wave to the people waiting nearby to attack. Of course, they too can see the gate being opened, but Jayashree will have a better, closer view. There's no room for error.

And yet an error does take place. The large iron gate is opened after some delay, and without the expected commotion. Jayashree waves, but it is a signal to hold off rather than attack. The team waiting at a distance does not read the signal correctly. Seeing the gate being opened and Jayashree waving, one group attacks the guards' barracks instantly, while the other charges at the gate. As planned. The roads shake under the explosion of powerful bombs. The smell of gunpowder fills the air.

Also as planned, as soon as they hear the bombs, a group of prisoners races out of Ward No. 7 towards the gate. The prisoners in the cells follow them. The guard on duty at the cells is injured trying to stop them. Goutam, Bablu and Bijon grab his stick and beat him to the ground. But, intent on escape, the maddened group of prisoners are astonished as they approach the gate. The wooden gate on this side, through which they have to pass to reach the main gate, has not been opened. It is standing in place like a giant exclamation mark. And Porimal, Ashu, Kalyan, even the thirty-odd other prisoners who should have been there, are nowhere to be seen.

Those who believe in destiny will call the failure of such a meticulously planned mission nothing but fate. Perhaps the gods of luck are not as favourably disposed towards the Naxals as they are towards Bireshwar Mukherjee the jailer. The outcome is inevitable.

It all began the night before. When all the prisoners had been locked up in their wards and cells. No one was supposed to know what was going on in the world beyond. As was his practice, the jail doctor was doing the rounds of the wards and cells to find out if anyone was ill. After the cells and Ward No. 7, he arrived at Ward No. 10 to discover that the condition of the bronchitis patient Sudhanshushekhar had suddenly worsened. He was finding it difficult to breathe. 'So many of you,' the doctor snarked. 'So many of you here. All of you. You couldn't bring him to the hospital? Couldn't bring him?'

'We told the guard many times,' said one of the prisoners. 'He refused to unlock the door. What can we do?'

'You couldn't even have sent word to me?'

'How could we? The gates are all locked.'

'Animals, animals everywhere. A man's dying. Dying. And we – all these guards, these jamadars, these officers, yes, even these officers – everyone's become inhuman. Animals, all. Animals. Even tigers in the zoo will be ashamed of them. Even tigers. In the zoo.'

Not that the doctor went back after his lecture. He located the jamadar, got him to unlock the door, and took Sudhanshushekhar to the hospital. But then getting a patient into the hospital doesn't cure him. You need medicines. There were no medicines in the jail hospital. So his condition deteriorated.

The doctor was not a man to give up. In the morning, he personally got all the necessary orders and permissions and made arrangements on his own initiative. There was no obstacle now to have Sudhanshushekhar transferred to a proper hospital. But red tape was still red tape, and the patient was not a minister's relative. He was an anti-national. So the ambulance did not arrive till one-thirty in the afternoon.

Some knew of Sudhanshushekhar's illness, but not everyone. Those who knew did not give it much importance. He had been taken away when ill, or rather, because of his illness. He had not been well ever since his arrival in jail. He had suffered from breathing problems earlier too, and recovered each time. So there was nothing special about it...

Some people do notice the ambulance when it arrives to take him away, but those who are directly associated with the plan are so charged up that they do not realise the hazard it poses.

Porimal and the rest have just emerged from the wire-mesh rooms after their meetings and are waiting outside the wooden gate. A guard says, 'Maal thodi der mein milega. Go into amdani for now. You'll get your things a little later. Let the ambulance go out.'

This is the rule. No prisoner is supposed to be nearby when the main gate is opened. Everyone is put into lock-up or, at the very least, taken ten yards away. Even if the rule is relaxed for the others, there is no surprise in the fact that it is followed stringently in the case of Naxals.

Now what? They can attack the guard, who is within reach, but that will only make things worse. The wooden gate is still locked.

So they retreat. Let the ambulance leave. Those who have been clustered around the case-table, waiting for their meetings, have already been locked up. The three of them are pushed in there as well, after which the guard locks the door. The ambulance arrives a little later. It is taking Sudhanshushekhar to a proper hospital outside the jail.

Bhojon Biswas unlocks the gate to let the ambulance out. The Naxals waiting outside are confused by the sight of the gate being opened. They follow their plan.

Bhojon is caught unprepared by the continuous explosions and the smell of gunpowder and smoke. But he gathers his wits quickly. Swiftly closing the gate and locking it, he races into the jailer's office. The splinters from the bombs will not find him now.

When the members of the action squad see an ambulance racing away and the gates being closed quickly, they realise their calculations have gone wrong. Not knowing what to do now, they disperse and make their escape.

The prisoners are caught like rats in a trap. All of them have evacuated Ward No. 7 and rushed to the main gate. But the way forward is blocked. And each and every prison guard is charging at them, their sticks raised. Porimal and Ashu know who will try to stop them. But they don't know whether Bhagoban is the right person for the job now.

The materials godown is next to the case-table. And next to it, the coal godown. Bhagoban is standing there. The man who was known as Bhagoban the thief till yesterday. Whose spine has bent under continuous assault by fellow humans. Who can no longer stand upright. Whose right arm hangs at an angle like a shovel. The scrawny figure of Bhagoban, less than five feet in height, stands like a mountain. Which cannot be crossed easily. A loaded revolver is glinting in his hand.

Not with a battlefield roar but in his usual servile tone he says, 'Shepai babura jikhene achho, shikhenei thako. Stay where you are, all you guards. Don't come this way. I'll shoot if you do. Look what I've got. It's a real gun, not a toy. Same as the police have.' He fires a shot. The man who is usually attacked by everyone makes the first move today.

Inside amdani, Ashu and Porimal are distraught. Everything's gone wrong. No hope. They'll have to die like rats. There's no way out. No one knows where the guard on duty here has escaped. The keys are with him. Kalyan pulls out his gun and tosses it to their friends rushing around outside. Let them use it to defend themselves as long as they can. Using the gun in here is useless.

'The ladder,' a helpless Porimal screams at Bijon. 'Use the electrician's ladder to scale the wall. Maybe some of you can get out that way.'

Bijon and Bablu run to prop up the ladder against the wall. But the panic-stricken prisoners are in disarray. Someone has to hold on to the base of a ladder for someone else to climb it. No one is ready to do that. Everyone wants to be the first to get out. The ladder becomes top-heavy. No one is holding it in place. It is toppled. This keeps happening. Some people are injured from their falls.

The watchtower is two hundred metres away from the spot where the ladder has been set against the wall. The sentry on duty there has realised what the prisoners are trying to do. And what he must do. Hitting a target two hundred metres away with a .303 rifle is not difficult. All it needs is willpower and a quelling of the rebelling heart.

Twenty-six guards are blowing their whistles for their lives. The pagla-ghanti is ringing at the gate. The warning sounds of the siren are spreading everywhere. The hyenas are waiting for the gates to be opened.

ELEVEN

Five dead bodies are lying on the portico outside the hospital. Unrecognisable. Pulverised faces. The number of the dead will rise. Two dozen are wounded, groaning. Three or four of them won't survive beyond a few hours. There are no medicines in the hospital. No trained workers to bandage the injured or provide any medical support. The dead and wounded alike are lying in a heap.

Although the alarm bells have stopped ringing, the guards are still seething with anger. They're scouring the wards and cells, looking for someone to teach a lesson. It's not just Naxals now, any prisoner who refused to comply with instructions earlier is being targeted. Since it has been proven that the Naxals were in cahoots with other prisoners, there's nothing to stop the guards.

All prisoners are supposed to run back to their wards as soon as the pagla-ghanti rings, and sit in pairs in a long row. That's the rule. Not taking one's position or not sitting down are signs of defiance. The guards are entitled to clobber them if that happens. The prisoners have been sitting in rows for four hours now. No one knows how much longer they will have to stay this way. The wards are being unlocked one by one and people are being picked out and taken outside. Their next destination is the hospital portico.

The sun is about to set, bathing the sky in the colour of blood. The earth will be devoured by darkness soon. All bloodstains will be removed under its cover. The odour of blood will be buried under bleaching powder. Human blood has a sharp smell, and countless seeds of life. New life springs from these drops of blood when they sink into the soil. A new fervour. Vengefulness. They will ensure that not a sign of any of this remains.

A breathless silence reigns over the jail now. Thousands of prisoners are squatting with their heads sunk into their shoulders, trembling, weeping like lambs about to be slaughtered. There's no sound to their weeping. Only saline sobs. Only a desperate shrieking can be heard somewhere. 'I'm dying. Oh god, I'm dying.'

A battalion of forces with rifles have surrounded the jail. No one is allowed to go within two hundred yards of the premises. Newspaper reporters and photographers are trying to collect as much information as they can from a distance.

The jail office is spilling over with people. A team of senior bureaucrats has arrived. They are wise and composed individuals who will embark on an inspection of the premises after having their tea, coffee, Coca-Cola, and taking a short rest. Since the situation is under control, since no one has escaped, there is no need for hasty action.

A plump officer, sporting an onyx ring, takes a pinch of mouth-freshener and tells the jailer, 'You're a very lucky man, Bireshwar-babu. Considering how they'd planned it, it would have been very difficult to stop them. Anyway, we must go to the spot now. Tell the guards to stop. Enough.'

'Yes, sir,' the jailer answers like an obedient schoolboy.

'And I hope things are as I wanted.'

'What things, sir?'

'There mustn't be more than eight dead.'

'Six so far, sir. But, sir, many of them are injured. Might exceed your number. Given the situation, it was impossible to keep an accurate count.'

'How many rounds were fired?'

'About a hundred and fifty.'

'Prepare a press report. It should say five rounds. The ones without bullet marks should be said to have died when they fell off the ladder. All right?'

'Yes, sir.'

'All right, let's go to the spot.'

A team of nine or ten officers sets off for the hospital. Their rank demands that the main gate be opened for them. But protocol cannot be maintained today. All of them enter with their heads bowed. Bhojon Biswas is still on gate duty. The officer with the onyx ring pats his shoulder. In other words, well done! There would have been a disaster if you hadn't managed to close the gate on time. His action makes it clear to the other guards and the jamadar that the touch of the onyx will open the door to good fortune for Bhojon. No one can come between him and a promotion now.

The officer goes past the main gate to stop in front of the field where it all happened. Torn slippers, blood-spattered clothes everywhere. Brown bloodstains on the earth. The grass flattened in the shape of human beings as their bodies were being dragged across it.

He walks up to the wall. Where the ladder had been propped up. Red streaks on its whitewashed surface. One long narrow smear going down all the way. Some flesh adhering to the wall in one place. A few strands of hair. Someone's head had been pounded against the wall. Telltale signs.

After inspecting the wall, he returns to amdani. The prisoners had put up some resistance here, using plates and glasses as missiles to stop the guards. The resistance didn't last long. The floor looks as though buckets of blood have been emptied on it.

'Isn't this where Bir Bahadur was injured?' the officer asks the jailer.

'Yes, sir. He wasn't well, but he rushed up all the same.'

'How many warders injured?'

'Five, sir. Bir Bahadur is in critical condition.'

'Please ensure no effort is spared in treating the warders,' the officer instructs a colleague standing next to him.

'Yes, sir,' the colleague responds. 'They're being given the best possible treatment. Dr Basu is looking after them.'

The officer moves on. The cells lie ahead of him. They're empty now. Their occupants are all lying on the floor of the portico outside the hospital. A few are inside. Not all of them have died yet. But they will. Some of them had tried to escape before too. This was their second infringement. There was no assurance they wouldn't try a third time if they survived. The authorities did not want to take a chance.

After inspecting the cells, the officer walks towards the hospital. All the activities are centred here now. The mad doctor is running about even more madly. The officer glares at him in a fury. He does not approve of a government employee taking care of seditious anti-national conspiring murderers with such zeal. What is the use of ministering to them? Let them die. But he does not tell the doctor as much. Nor does he ask any questions. He only observes the doctor's efforts. He even sees what most people's eyes cannot see. There have been a lot of rumours about this doctor. He's a principled man, doesn't shirk his duty, doesn't take bribes. There is no alternative to being suspicious of a government employee who is so honest. He must have been bitten by the dog of ideology. The rabid poison is spreading through his veins.

'Can we not see the doctor playing a role in today's incident?' the officer asks himself.

'Yes, and a major one at that,' he answers himself.

'What are the reasons for drawing this conclusion?'

'Several. First, his weakness for Naxal prisoners. Many people have indicated that he does not treat them the same way he does other prisoners. He tours the wards personally, asking about their problems. Why? It can only mean he supports the activities of Naxals. He is their well-wisher. It is by virtue of being a well-wisher that he is implicated in today's conspiracy. Take the Naxal prisoner with bronchitis. No one is claiming he is not ill. He is. But he was used to hatch a plot for the jailbreak.'

'Was that done with the doctor's knowledge?'

'It's too soon to tell. But it isn't necessarily an incorrect assumption. No one knows what a person really thinks, and how he might act. What if we assume that the doctor is an equal conspirator, that it was on his suggestion that Sudhanshushekhar exaggerated his illness and was admitted to the hospital. I'm terming it an exaggeration because the guard on ward duty did not report any serious illness last night. It was the doctor who did it. Is this a doctor's job? Does doing something beyond the call of duty not prove that the doctor had taken the initiative to create an opportunity for them? Using the patient as a pretext, he had asked for the ambulance at the precise time the Naxals were to be near the gate. As soon as the gate would be opened for the ambulance to leave, the Naxals lying in wait nearby would lay siege on it. One gate was open already, they would use bombs and guns to force the other one open. At the same time, the rest of the prisoners would attack the guards. Then all of them would escape. Wasn't this the plan? Yes, it was. And the doctor knew it. But he's not being charged with conspiracy immediately. An enquiry is required. Followed by necessary steps.'

The officer glances at the inert bodies on the floor. They look like lumps of flesh, not humans. Mangled and gruesome. Brains leaking out of cracked skulls. Flies swarming around them. These will lie here for some more time. Only after the darkness deepens will they be added to the heap of corpses at some other hospital.

The officer enters the hospital, stepping over the bodies carefully so that he gets no blood on his feet. The hospital is equipped with beds for four or five patients. There are many more today. All of them groaning on the floor. Some with bullet wounds, some with fractures and injuries from being beaten up. The doctor is bandaging them one by one. He looks at the officer without stopping work. His eyes are pleading. 'There's nothing I can do. Nothing I can do. No medicines, no bandages, not even enough cotton-wool.'

'But you're there.' The officer gestures with his eyes, as though he's said something funny. 'Do what you can, do as much as you can. Leave the rest to god.'

'Six or seven of them need to be sent to a proper hospital right now. Need to be sent right now.'

'Don't be impatient. Arrangements are being made. Naturally it'll take some time.'

'By then, sir...'

'By when?'

'Nothing.' The doctor focuses on what he's doing. 'Animals,' he mutters in his head. 'Animals, all of them!'

After his visit to the hospital, the officer goes to the chauka. There's no activity or hubbub here now. The place is desolate. The fires in the clay ovens have gone out. The pans on them are empty. Not a single prisoner is alive in the jail right now. All of them have died of fear. Their only prayer now is: let nothing more happen, let things be normal again.

The next stop after the chauka is Ward No. 2. Room No. 7 in this ward is in a desperate state. There's not a person here who has not been beaten up. All of them are sitting in rows, writhing in pain from contusions and injuries. They know from experience that the torture on them will continue for quite some time.

The officer pauses at the door to Room No. 7 for a look. A cruel smile appears on his face. 'Not trying to escape anymore, my heroes? Why so quiet now? Try. If you don't succeed at first, try again. Best of luck.'

He returns to his chair by the case-table. The darkness has become dense by now. A gentle breeze is blowing from the south, like someone's warm breath. A powerful searchlight is watching over everything from the tower like a one-eyed monster.

Now the officer walks up to the main gate. The secret of a long life is avoiding tension and staying cheerful all the time. He does not allow anything ugly to sully his thoughts. In the office he drinks a Coca-Cola. Then he leaves, escorted by police vans.

TWELVE

The night is impenetrably black now, deep and desolate. A nocturnal bird is wailing on the parapet of a house somewhere. Like a motherless child. Its cries in the darkness have created an atmosphere of fear. Bhagoban has just regained consciousness. He had collapsed from the blow on his head. And now, like the lamp that flares for the last time before going out, Bhagoban has awakened. He has no pain in his body anymore, he's not suffering. He feels no sorrow or remorse or regret. His heart is light, unburdened, calm. He reaches out to feel someone lying next him. It's impossible to identify the person. He's covered in bandages. There's a rumbling in his throat. His chest is probably congested. 'Can you hear me? Shunti paartechho?' Bhagoban says softly. There's no reply. Replying is impossible. All that's left of him is the rumbling. Soon the figure will fall silent. And he will be transformed from a human being to a corpse.

Pagla Daktar has not yet left. His work isn't done. It will only be done when the dead and the wounded are shifted to appropriate places. Arrangements are being made, the doctor has been told.

Hearing Bhagoban speak, the doctor rises from his chair and goes up to him. 'What, you're alive? Still alive? Are you indestructible? Want some water?'

'Who are you?' mutters Bhagoban.

'Want some water?' Without waiting for a reply, the doctor pours some water down Bhagoban's throat. There's no sign of his normal antipathy for thieves and pickpockets.

It was a long time ago. He had completed ten years on the job, absorbed in his duties as a doctor. A patient was just a patient, not a criminal.

He was on his way to Bowbazar to buy his daughter some jewellery for her wedding. Unwilling to be corrupt, he hadn't managed to save much, and had been forced to borrow money from his friends. He was on the train, with all the money in a bag. When he got off at Sealdah Station, he discovered the bag had been sliced open and all the money taken away. Paying for the wedding was a nightmare. The bitter memory of anger and humiliation had never left him. He used to say regretfully, 'The people I worked for all my life, all my life I worked for them, they're the ones who did this to me. I never imagined, never imagined they could, honestly, never thought it possible.' Which is why he cannot tolerate thieves. But now, giving Bhagoban a drink of water, not the job of a doctor – he is overwhelmed.

'I didn't imagine that's what you were up to, that's what you were up to secretly, I never imagined,' he said.

'Not that I succeeded.'

'At what?'

'That I...'

Bhagoban is gasping. He's finding it difficult to breathe. He won't be drawing many more breaths. 'Will the papers write about me?' he asks.

'Of course! All the papers. Bangla Hindi English all. They'll all have the news. Pictures.'

'Everyone will know of me.'

'Everyone. There will be a storm in the Assembly.'

Bhagoban sighs gratefully. 'Taali aar kono kawshto naai. No more pain. I don't care what happens now.'

The doctor is irritated. 'So you gave your life for fame. Just for fame. Nothing but fame. You're an ass. A complete ass. Just to be famous? How can anyone? You let yourself be nabbed with a loaded gun. Didn't kill anyone. Not one. You'd die anyway. If you're going to die, take some of them out too. Kill a dozen of them. Kill a dozen then die. If you're going to die anyway, kill some of them first. Died like an ass. You're an idiot. An idiot.'

Bhagoban doesn't speak. He cannot speak. Finally, after a long time, he says in a voice from a distant mountain peak, 'I could have, daktar-babu. Could have killed a few. But my heart wouldn't let me. My finger wouldn't move. Kill whom? I'd only kill people like me. Poor, hopeless. They've left their families behind to labour in jail. Isn't that what we do here, hard labour? One night, it was raining so hard, lightning and thunder. The storm broke trees, not a soul anywhere. Just one old sentry on wall duty standing there, not fearing for his life. For what, daktar-babu? Just for a meal. How can I kill another poor man? I couldn't do it. But it's true, if they hadn't just stood there, if they'd come this way, I wouldn't have had a choice. When I saw that was impossible, what could I do? Threw the gun away.'

Bhagoban stops. It's time. He will fall silent for ever now. The doctor asks him no more questions. Away from prying eyes, with nobody around, no one knows why, the doctor brings his palms together in a gesture of reverence to Bhagoban.

If these thousands of fearless young Naxals can succeed with their revolution one day, and a researcher like John Reed writes the history of these stormy, tumultuous days, will he find something in the story of Bhagoban Sardar, the unknown thief who died of torture and neglect in the darkness of the jail, something that can make his pen weep? Will he pause in wonder?

The only witness to the existence of such a man is Pagla Daktar. No one else.

The doctor doesn't have to wait much longer. A van covered with black mesh arrives at the hospital gate. Four demons jump out, bare-bodied, reeking of country liquor. Corpse-bearers. Murda-farash. Picking up the dead bodies by their arms and legs, the four demons throw them into the van one at a time. Loaded with eight bodies, the van leaves as it came. Two more vans arrive, to be loaded with the eighteen severely wounded prisoners. Two armed police vans escort them away.

Time to go home. As he leaves, the doctor sees the wall being whitewashed. A pump is spewing out water to remove the bloodstains.

THIRTEEN

Three months have passed. Exactly ninety days. The measurement of days-months-years-time appears differently to individuals. To the prisoner counting the days to freedom after twenty years in jail, a month is like ten years, it never ends. To the prisoner on death row counting down to execution, time is a rocket, streaking through the sky, bringing his days on earth to an end.

To Bireshwar Mukherjee the jailer, time seems to have come to an abrupt stop. Yesterday, today, tomorrow – the past, the present, the future – are all tedious and impossible to tell from one another. Rounds in the morning, some hours in the office, read the papers, go on more rounds, home for lunch and a nap, more rounds in the afternoon, some more hours in the office, home to watch TV, eat dinner, sleep.

For some time the jail was caught in chaos, taut with tension. It has dissipated with extraordinary speed. There are too many crises around the country for the authorities to focus on a single incident. Having completed the enquiry into the attempted jailbreak at lightning speed, they have homed in on other things. Excitement has made way for lassitude and exhaustion.

This morning, too, the jailer has appeared at the entrance to the prison as he does every day at the wailing of the siren. Walking between two rows of guards, he has reached the iron gates. The guards have clicked their heels. The jamadar has raised his sword in salute. Suddenly Jamadar Raghubir Tiwari rushes up, panting. 'Sahib, gajab ho gaya. The strangest thing has happened.'

'Now what?' The jailer is alert in an instant.

'Bandiswala came last night.'

'Bandiswala!'

'Yes, sir.'

'How do you know Bandiswala aaya tha? Who saw him?'

'He's left proof. Written things on the wall.'

'Written what?'

'I can't read Bangla.'

'Which wall?'

'Where the Naxals died.'

'Let's go.'

The bandaged ghost has been harassing them constantly. Does he never get exhausted? There was no sign of him during those few days when the trouble with the Naxals erupted. Now that things are back to normal, he has resurfaced. Bireshwar Mukherjee's heart skips several beats when he arrives at the thirty-foot wall next to amdani, the wall on which Rajat's blood had been sprayed. The man who was not shaken even by the sight of eight fresh dead bodies crumples on seeing the wall. The graffiti makes him feel as though someone has just riddled him with bullets.

With the gate locked, they had put up a ladder against the wall as the last resort. The ladder toppled to the ground several times because of their hurry to climb it. By the time their common sense reasserted itself, the sentry on duty in the tower had become alert. As soon as Rajat reached the top, the sentry had pulled the trigger. He had no trouble hitting the target from just two hundred metres away. As Rajat's body was hurtling to the ground, his feet were caught in the rungs of the ladder. So his corpse dangled in mid-air, close to the wall. The same ladder that kept slipping earlier was now steady, no one knew why. Dripping from Rajat's bullet-riddled chest, the blood took on the shape of India's map as it flowed down the wall.

There was a fresh fusillade. This time there was no need to aim. Since there was a mass of people, the bullets were bound to hit someone. Three or four were felled by the random firing. The rest ran behind amdani to save themselves. Some of them tried to return to their cells. But by then the nature of the battle had changed. The guards had started killing. And then there was a grand festival of death across the jail.

All the bloodstains were removed that same night with lime and bleaching powder. The wall next to amdani was whitewashed too. Now a fresh set of letters, words, sounds, has appeared on it.

Birer e raktosrot, matar e osrudhara
Er joto mulyo shey ki dhorar dhuloy hobe hara?

The hero's blood, the mother's precious tears
Will they all go dry in the dust at our feet?

These are not lines of poetry, these are cannonballs of fire. A vow to wage total war, an oath written in letters of blood. Forgetting the dignity of his position, the jailer shrieks, 'Who wrote this?'

'Everyone suspects Bandiswala.'

'You think you can fool me? Bandiswala my arse! I've seen his case history. He was from Bihar. Illiterate. Angootha chhap. Thumb impression. Did he become a pundit after dying? A Tagore scholar? This is no ghost, this is a human being.'

'Sahib, no prisoner can go up to the wall,' says the jamadar deferentially. 'And besides, they were all in lock-up when this was written. How can it have been a human being?'

'What about the guards? Could be one of them. Who was on duty here?'

'Sahib, all the guards know writing on the jail wall is illegal,' said the jamadar. 'They can be suspended for it. Who will take the risk?'

No one will. The jailer knows it. But who can do such a thing without being seen by the guards? Who? In that case, was it…? But how can he indulge such an unscientific notion now, in the twentieth century, the age of reason? How can he believe such a thing? Still, he isn't imagining the words written in large black letters on the wall in front of him. They're real.

Riven by doubt, the jailer looks behind him. Not just Raghubir Tiwari, even some of the prison guards who have earned a name for their bravery are standing there pale and sweating. Everyone is trembling in fear. The jailer does what is most obvious. He orders the jamadar to have the slogans wiped off. 'I want to see the wall clean on my way back from my rounds,' he says.

The jamadar instructs the guard standing next to him, 'Amdani se incharge ko bulao. Call the amdani incharge. Tell him to bring a bucket of water and rags.' The last prisoner who was in charge at amdani has got bail. The new one is named Gajendra Singh. Accused of double murder. He gets into a state of panic on receiving the orders. Given his strength and courage, he can beat up half a dozen convicts if instructed. He has done it, in fact. But to go up against a ghost rather than a human being makes his knees tremble. His blood runs cold.

A prisoner had once fallen foul of Bandiswala. 'All lies,' he had said. 'Bandiswala has no powers. If he couldn't harm us when alive, how can he do anything to us when dead. Let him do something to show us if he can.' He was dead within a week. No storm, not even a wind. He was found with an electric wire wound around his neck. He was returning from the chauka.

Gajendra is shaking with terror. He has not one but two charges of 302 on him. He'll have to spend his entire life breaking rocks in jail if convicted. You need blessings, not rage, from demons in such moments of crisis.

Putting on a forlorn expression, he says, 'My session trials are about to start. Please don't ask me to do all this.'

'What can go wrong if you wipe off the slogans.' The jamadar tries to give him courage. 'It will be fine, just do it. Pochh de.'

'Nahin, bada baba. Please forgive me, sir. Get someone else to do it.' Gajendra is on the verge of tears.

Now the jamadar is angry. 'Are you going to follow my orders or not? I'll strip you off your post.'

'Go ahead. Lock me up in a cell in handcuffs. Do whatever you please. But don't make me fight with Bandiswala. He will eat me up.'

Intimidation does not work. You can only intimidate those who are afraid of humans. Never mind Gajendra, no prisoner will be willing to risk the wrath of Bandiswala.

Suddenly the jamadar remembers that a set of new prisoners has come today. It will be easy to get one of them to do it. They don't know anything about Bandiswala. So that's what he does. 'Fetch two of the new ones from the case-tables,' he orders Gajendra, who complies. They clean the wall with water and the rags.

The jailer arrives to inspect the wall. The marks that sent a chill down his spine have been wiped off for now, but they remain like festering wounds in his heart. Can the value of the hero's blood be obliterated from people's minds just because it has been cleaned off a wall?

He returns to his office, exhausted. He's panting. Something is crumbling inside him. Who knows what new message will appear on the wall tomorrow or the day after?

Deputy Jailer Mohinimohon comes up to him with his beady eyes and nostrils packed with snuff. 'What's the matter, sir? Why are you sweating? Aren't you feeling well?'

'No, just a terrible incident. Shocking.'

Terrible incident? The deputy jailer is inquisitive. Slumping on a chair, he says, 'What is it, sir?' Having heard the whole thing, he says, 'Yes, sir, shocking. Do you think this is Bandiswala's doing?'

'I'm confused. What do I say? So far as I know he was illiterate.'

After a pause the jailer continues, 'The prisoners are locked in their wards. Even if the guards had done something silly like this earlier, they wouldn't take the risk now. Bandiswala is illiterate. Whose work is this? You know what I think?' He laughs sarcastically. 'Must be Naxal ghosts.'

'What are you saying, sir?!'

'Trees don't grow on fallow ground. Like deserts. But where the earth is fertile, all it needs is for a seed to fall. Some soils are suitable for certain trees. Our soil and environment in the jail here is suitable for growing ghosts. I suspect Bandiswala is alone no more. He has companions.'

'You're joking, sir,' says the deputy jailer, looking hurt.

'Why do you say that?'

'You claim there's no such thing as souls or spirits. And now you're saying...'

'People change their beliefs, don't they? I've revised my original view. I think this is the handiwork of Naxal ghosts.'

The deputy jailer has got a chance to show off his knowledge to his boss. He won't let it go. 'Even if you accept the truth of ghosts, sir, those lines were not written by ghosts or at least Naxal ghosts. Naxals are dead set against Tagore. They call him a bourgeois poet. I believe they have even vandalised his statues. Tagore-haters cannot suddenly turn into Tagore-lovers after death. People don't change their qualities, for good or for bad, after they die. At most they can ebb and flow, depending on the positions of the stars and the planets. It's definitely not the ghost of dead Naxals who have done this deed.'

Then who has?

They have to find out.

FOURTEEN

There's a guard in this jail named Bhojon Biswas. Middle-aged, his hair greying. Thin, dark, wears high-powered glasses. Everyone knows he's a fortunate man. He didn't have to move a finger during the storm that blew over the jail a few days ago. He neither had to face the loaded revolvers of the Naxals, nor did he have to crack open anyone's skull. He was effectively in the safest, most secure of places. There was just the one task he had to perform, which was to close the gates. It was enough to make him a hero. The IG (Prison) congratulated him personally. He has been lavishly praised in the press, with his photograph being published. There's talk of his being recommended for a bravery medal on Republic Day. A promotion is coming any day now. His colleagues are burning with envy. All of them are bursting with regret at not having been assigned gate duty that day. Bhojon was not supposed to have been there. It was only because Bir Bahadur had fallen ill that he was picked.

But Bir Bahadur was not really sick. He had given an excuse. He wanted to drink and laze all day. Now he sighs at Bhojon's luck. What an opportunity he has lost.

But no matter what others think, Bhojon considers himself unfortunate and unhappy. None of these accolades can bring a smile to his face. A secret agony eats away at him. In a particularly painful moment, he bares his heart to a close friend. 'I'm thinking of giving up this job.'

'But why?'

'I'm not enjoying it anymore.'

'What will you do instead?'

'I have two bighas of lands. I'll buy two more. Be a farmer.'

'Can you really give up a job for farming?'

'Why not. My father was a farmer. It's in my blood.'

'That's true. But you're not getting any younger. It's hard work.'

'Maybe. Still a thousand times better than killing people. Fresh as flowers, all those boys. All dead. They'd laugh and sing, so cheerful all the time. All of them beaten to death like snakes. The empty cells make me cry when I'm on duty there. There was a boy named Bijon. Just like my Pujon. When I remember his face, I feel like screaming.'

'Be strong. Don't do anything impulsively. You didn't kill anyone. It was their fate. Why are you upset? Not your fault.'

'Not my fault, but my fault too. It's a matter of direct and indirect responsibility. Someone who works in an ammunitions factory doesn't kill anyone directly, but indirectly he does. He knows what he makes. People can rationalise, but that man is connected to every bullet that lodges itself in someone's chest. He is responsible too.'

'If you look at it that way, everyone is responsible.'

'Perhaps. But I don't like it here anymore. Bijon and his friends said no work that makes you unhappy is worth doing. My son used to say anything that you repent having done is a sin. There's no joy in what I do, and I repent it too.'

Bhojon's friend is surprised to hear the words 'my son used to say'. 'Used to' is fine for Bijon, but why for his son? Why not 'my son says'?

Bhojon hasn't used the past tense consciously. It has come to him naturally. He hasn't told anyone in Calcutta about 'says' having become 'used to say'. He hasn't been able to. But in unguarded moments, the cruel truth spurts from his unconscious mind like blood from a wound.

Bhojon returned to his workplace heartbroken the last time he went home. He didn't meet Pujon during the short leave he had managed to get with great difficulty. He has no close relatives back home in the village. All distant cousins. The letters they wrote in response to his queries made him anxious. The boy was wandering around as though lost. Unkempt hair, unshaven. Apparently he had formed a music group. No one knew what sort of songs. Neither folk songs nor devotional – apparently it was called gana-sangeet. People's songs. What was the use of all this? No one paid to listen. Waste of effort. After things quietened down in the jail, Bhojon got three days' casual leave. Two and a half hours on the train, an hour on the bus, forty-five minutes on a van-rickshaw. Finally, his own village. The house looked like no one had set foot there in a long time. Weeds everywhere. A kingdom of bloodsucking leeches. Insects, frogs, snakes.

Bhojon's family was not one of the original settlers in this area. His father and some others had drifted here after the partition. With the little money he had been given, he bought some land, put up a house, and began farming. Like everyone else. Bhojon got some education. He went to Calcutta to see if it could earn him a living. His mother's brother got him a job as a prison guard. Back then you didn't need to know anybody important to get a job with the police or in the military. If you were healthy and literate, you had to queue up on the appointed date at the appointed time. Serving officers picked out new recruits.

When he went home, Bhojon's first task was to look for Pujon. Where should he start? Who would give him news of his son? He was at his wits' end. That was when the village chowkidar arrived to chat with him. 'When did you arrive, dada? Oh, today. How are you? Don't ask about the village. All peace and quiet is gone. Nothing but thefts and robberies, stabbings and murders everywhere. And on top of that, the party people. Everyone's trying to kill someone. I was at the police station. How do I tell you, dada... four corpses in the canal. Killed and their bodies dumped in the water. Couldn't bear to look at them. Same age as our Habul and your Pujon. There are no humans anywhere, all devils. And everything for the party. Parents don't matter, elders don't matter, gods and goddesses don't matter. They don't believe in religion, caste, anything. No wonder things are so wretched here. Anyway, what news of Pujon? We hardly see him. Where does he live?'

Bhojon set off for the police station at once. An invisible magnet drew him to the single-storied structure twenty-two miles away. Arrangements were being made to load the four corpses on two van-rickshaws and send them for post-mortem. There was no way of identifying the mangled, battered, rotting bodies. Nor was there any way to find out why they had been killed so brutally. Bhojon didn't know why, but he felt their names were Porimal, Bijon, Bablu, Nemai, Kalyan, Ashu. It was impossible to be otherwise. The same disfigured, bloodied, mutilated bodies...

Bhojon had forgotten food and drink in his headlong rush to the police station twenty-two miles away, driven by the same fear that makes every father's heart tremble when their son isn't back home on time, forcing him to consider visiting the hospital, the police station, the jail, the mortuary. To quell his anxiety, Bhojon went up to the officer-in-charge.

'Who are they, sir?'

The officer had a sense of humour. 'Can't you see? Corpses.'

'Have they been identified?'

'Corpses have no identities these days. Only serial numbers. Probably thousand eighty-five, eighty-six.'

'Sir, I...'

'Yes? Are you the father of 1085?'

'There's been no news of my son for a long time.'

'Like many others.'

'May I see their faces?'

'They have no faces. Identical. Even if one of them is your son, you won't be able to tell. They've been under water for ten days... Why do you think your son's among them?'

'I don't know. It's the innocent boys who're getting murdered these days. That's why.'

It wasn't easy, but after a lot of pleading the officer agreed, setting a price of only twenty rupees. 'Not me, give it to that fellow there. They have to handle these rotting corpses. Let them make a little money.'

The officer had said he wouldn't be able to recognise his son. But Bhojon did. A distant relative had written, beard, unkempt hair. Those were the clues. And not just the first one, even the second, third and fourth corpses were Pujon's.

Bhojon returned from the police station with the knowledge lurking secretly in his breast. It's still secret. He hasn't told anyone...

Bhojon has just come back from work. He was on duty all night. He has cleared his bowels, eaten a breakfast of doi and chinre and is lying down for a nap. Suddenly he is told that the jailer has sent for him. The messenger is Shukumar. He has a look of suppressed elation. 'What's the matter, why the urgent summons?' asks Bhojon. 'Has anything happened?'

'You're the golden boy now,' Shukumar laughs. 'Bhagwan jab deta hai, chhappad phaadke deta hai. Everything's coming your way. The promotion doesn't seem too far away. Maybe the IG's letter is here. They've called you to hand it over. Take a transfer if it's a promotion, okay? If you can move to Central Jail, laal hoye jaabe. You'll be rich in two years.'

Bhojon has never hankered for a promotion. He's actually thinking of quitting. He saunters over to the office.

The jailer, deputy jailer and security officer are deep in discussion. As soon as Bhojon appears, the security officer asks, 'Where were you posted last night?'

Bhojon feels it's a loaded question. 'You know very well, sir. You made the chart.'

'You were supposed to have been at the hospital. Were you there?'

'Where do you suppose I was if not there?'

'I want an answer, not a counter-question.'

'I was there.'

'Did you fall asleep?'

'Not for a moment.'

'Not for a moment. Then how did the slogans appear on the hospital wall? Who wrote them?'

'Slogans!'

'Go take a look. Then come back and explain.'

Bhojon hesitates.

'Go, Bhojon. See for yourself,' says the deputy jailer.

A message of hope is scrawled in large letters on the wall of the portico where the bodies of Porimal and the rest lay in neglect for over ten hours.

> Udayer pother shuni kaar baani
> Bhoy naai orey bhoy naai
> Nihsheshe praan je koribek daan
> Khoy naai taar khoy naai

On the road to dawn I hear a voice
Do not fear, oh, do not fear
There are some who'll give their entire lives
Death is not a word they will hear

Bhojon reads it. Some of the punctuation and spelling is wrong. But the use of colour on this particular wall is significant.

A faltu has appeared with the milk for the guards' tea. Reading the slogan, he says, 'Makes your blood boil, doesn't it Bhojon-da? Those who give their entire lives…my god.'

Bhojon returns to the gate. The security officer is no longer in the office. The clerk Shurjo-babu has arrived. 'Well, Bhojon-babu?' he asks. 'Any idea who wrote it?'

'The ghost, I think,' chuckles the jailer.

'This is no time for jokes, sir,' the deputy jailer tells him.

Bhojon looks at them in turn, trying to gauge their mood. Is there going to be an explosion?

The jailer continues, 'Why does this slogan-writing ghost fancy you so much, Bhojon? The duty chart shows last week too all the slogans appeared while you were on duty. And now it's happened again. What's going on?'

The security officer returns from wherever he'd gone. He's accompanied by a jamadar and a prison guard. The guard is carrying a brush and a can of paint. The security officer holds a volume of Tagore's selected poems. 'Didn't I tell you,' he says to the jailer. 'Here you are. What more proof do you want? I've long had my doubts.' Turning to Bhojon, he adds, 'We searched your quarters and found these. It wasn't hard getting in, the door was unlocked. I had to do it keeping the security of the jail in mind.' Tossing the volume of poetry on the desk, he wipes his forehead and exclaims, 'One incident after another is taking place in the jail, with the support of a section of the employees here. You can deny it if you wish. You can say the security officer is framing you, that those things were planted in your room.'

'They were all in my room.'

'So you admit writing all those things on the wall?'

'I do.'

'Why did you do it?'

'I wanted to.'

'Why did you want to?'

When Bhojon doesn't reply, the jailer says sternly, 'Out with it, Bhojon. You have to reply. Don't expect to get by without answering.'

Bhojon begins to speak. First softly, then louder. With a mixture of emotion, agitation, anger and aggression, he says, 'I wanted to protest. These lively bright young men were tortured in cold blood for four or five hours and then systematically killed. No one spoke up against this cruelty and violence. Who were these boys? They loved the country, they loved its people. They wanted to free these people from misery, from oppression, from deprivation. We labelled them violent, tortured them, killed them. If they were violent, is each of us an apostle incarnate of non-violence?'

There's silence in the office. No one says a word. The silence is so intense that the rattling of the guard's keys at the gate sounds like an assault on the ears. Bhojon continues speaking. 'I saw them closely, day after day. I spoke to them, came to know them. They were the exact opposite of the image that the government's propaganda machinery tried to create. Tomorrow if not today, whether they are victorious or not, the real history of these young men will be written. People will spit on our faces then. They will get the same respect that Bhagat Singh gets, that Khudiram Bose gets, that Benoy Bose and Badal Gupta and Dinesh Gupta get. I just atoned in a small way for my crime.' After he has finished speaking, the jailer says, 'I applaud your courage. I hope you will demonstrate the same courage in response to the show-cause notice.'

'You can count on it,' says Bhojon.

'In which case, you run the risk of being suspended indefinitely, even dismissed from your job.'

'I don't care.' Bhojon flings his answer at them and walks out of the gate in full sight of his thunderstruck colleagues. The wide road stretches out in front of him. Hundreds of people are walking along it. Standing among them, Bhojon Biswas feels he has just been released from jail after serving a life sentence. He tells himself what he used to tell the prisoners who walked free when he was on duty at the gate. 'Don't do anything that will bring you back here.'

ALSO BY MANORANJAN BYAPARI

Imaan enters Central Jail as an infant—in the arms of Zahura Bibi, his mother, who is charged with the murder of his father and who dies when he is six. He leaves twenty years later, having spent his time thus far shuttling between a juvenile home and prison. With no home to return to, Imaan ends up at the Jadavpur railway station, becoming a ragpicker on the advice of a consummate pickpocket.

The folk of the railside—rickshaw-pullers, scrap dealers, tea-stall owners, those who sell corpses for a little bit of money—welcome him into their fold, but the world of the free still baffles him. Life on the platform is disillusioning, and far more frightening than the jail he knew so well. This free world too is a prison, like the one he came from, only disconcertingly large. But no one went hungry in jail. And everyone had a roof over their heads.

Unable to cope in this odd world, Imaan wishes to return to the security of a prison cell. He is told that, while there is only one door out of prison, there are a thousand through which to return. Is Imaan—whose name means honesty, conscience—up to the task?

Written in Manoranjan Byapari's inimitable style, where irony and wry humour are never too far from bitter truths, this new novel is a searing exploration of the lives of the faceless millions who get by in our towns and cities, making it through one day at a time.

The first part of Byapari's extraordinary trilogy of novels begins in East Pakistan. It tells the story of little Jibon, who arrives at a refugee camp in West Bengal as an infant in the arms of his Dalit parents, who have escaped from the Muslim-majority nation. Deprived of the customary sweetness of a few drops of honey at birth, he grows up perpetually hungry for hot rice in the camp where the treatment meted out to dispossessed families like his is deplorable. Jibon runs away when he's barely thirteen to Calcutta because he's heard that money flies in the air in the big city. His wildly innocent imagination makes him believe that he can go out into the world, find work and bring back food for his starving siblings and clothes for his mother whose only sari is in tatters.

And once he leaves home, through the travels of this starving, bewildered but gritty boy, we witness a newly independent India as it grapples with communalism and grave disparities of all kinds.

This is a work of great brilliance and beauty.

'In evocative and imagery-rich writing, Manoranjan Byapari introduces us to the devastating realities of mid-twentieth-century India: hunger, caste violence, and communal hatred. Jibon's experiences in his tortured world remind us of the distance we have come, and how far we have yet to go.'
—Dr Shashi Tharoor

'Manoranjan Byapari is an outspoken, fearless and unapologetic writer. His writings seethe with anger and indignation, and *The Runaway Boy* is no different. It is a gut-wrenching account of caste atrocities, dirty politics and crippling poverty that no discerning reader should miss.'
—Hansda Sowvendra Shekhar

'*The Runaway Boy* is a piercing tale of human determination, shorn of hackneyed sentimentalism, and set in an unforgiving territory of death and desperation. Cuttingly frank, deeply political, and singular in feeling, this is an incandescent universe of long sufferings and small, fleeting joys. Manoranjan Byapari does not confirm abstract theories the better-fed cultivate about the poor; he holds up a mirror that reveals, instead, through the pangs of a boy seeking hot rice, a world that feasts on the soul, and where hell is not a faraway place as much as everyday reality.'
—Manu S. Pillai

The second part of this extraordinary trilogy takes us into the late '60s and early '70s when the rumblings of liberation grew louder in East Pakistan and refugees came pouring into India, seeking asylum in the camps of West Bengal. The Naxalite movement too was gathering momentum; the CPI(M), which had broken away from the Communist Party, itself split with the formation of the CPI(ML), and a bitter power tussle ensued between its factions and the ruling party led by Indira Gandhi. Amidst this bloody battle, we find a twenty-something Jibon in Calcutta, driven to rage by hunger, inequity and a naïve, contagious nationalistic fervour.

This burning torch of a novel is a compelling portrait of a youth negotiating the streets of Calcutta, looking to seize a life that is constantly denied to him.

'Manoranjan Byapari's epic narratives tell you more about our society than any number of studies by social theorists or political psychologists. Immersed in a world of caste violence and congenital poverty, here is fiction with the unmistakable ring of contemporary Indian history.'

—Jeet Thayil

'A remorseless account of Jibon's saga of survival. Haunted by hunger and disease in the deep forests of Dandakaranya. Caught between deadly party wars and police atrocities in a city torn apart by the Naxalite movement. But even in this harsh world, Jibon will experience the first tender stirrings of love and desire. A book that will shake you to the core.'

—Poonam Saxena

'In the shape of a novel, Manoranjan Byapari serves us a great outpouring of pain and a hundred fierce cries for justice. This book ought to be on syllabi across the country so we may better understand how structural violence works at the intersection of caste, class and law enforcement.'

—Annie Zaidi

www.ingramcontent.com/pod-product-compliance
Lightning Source LLC
LaVergne TN
LVHW010326070526
838199LV00065B/5674